THE PROGRAMMED PEOPLE

By
JACK SHARKEY

I0541445

ARMCHAIR FICTION
PO Box 4369, Medford, Oregon 97504

TO SOME IT SEEMED LIKE A PERFECT EXISTENCE...

Everything ran so smoothly that it seemed to define perfection. From the bright light of day to the Ultrablack, the faceless people who lived in "the hive" went about their carefully structured lives in seemingly blissful ignorance of their real ruler and the true history of their race. So it seemed highly improbable that one slender blonde girl could crack this powerful monolithic monstrosity— certainly without peril to her life.

The future of man seemed stark, and the hive was one place that no one ever left—alive. Join science fiction master Jack Sharkey as he takes you down a lonely road to a world of bleak expectations in this moving, well-done science fiction thriller.

FOR A COMPLETE SECOND NOVEL, TURN TO PAGE 111

CAST OF CHARACTERS

LLOYD BODGER, SR.
The Secondary Speakster of the Hive who kept a terrible secret—he could cause the destruction of the entire Hive.

LLOYD BODGER, JR.
He was a good, loyal Kinsman of the Hive, until he learned the horrible truth.

GRACE HORTON
She was the fiancée to Lloyd, Jr., but she would go only so far to protect him.

ANDREA CORBY
She knew the truth about the Hive, but how could she convince Lloyd, Jr. that all he believed in was a lie?

FREDRIC STANTON
The power-hungry President and Prime Speakster of the Hive, he knew what happened to those who went for "readjustment."

THE BRAIN
The computer that controlled the Hive, it did what it logically deduced was best for the Hive, even at the cost of human life.

CHAPTER ONE

UNDER the stark blue-white glow that glittered from hidden niches onto the faceted undersurface of the vast vaulted crystal dome, the people milled and jockeyed for position near the dais. There was still room to move about and select a standing-site; most of the heavy thronging was still at the entrances, the wide, squat arches giving egress to the fifteen block-long arcades that radiated from the center of the temple like the spokes of a gigantic wheel. Between the pillars that framed these arches, long unbroken walls served as firm backdrops for the Vote Boxes, twenty-five to a wall, three hundred seventy-five in all, to service a building that could hold five thousand.

Lloyd Bodger took a quick look at his wristwatch while there was still sufficient elbow-room to lift his arm. Two minutes till eight P.M. service began promptly on the hour. He gauged his nearness to the dais with a practiced eye, then let himself be wedged into place by the increasing pressure of urgent bodies about him. It would not do to remain in the rear of the hemispherical room, where he might lose some of the Speakster's words, words that might have direct bearing upon the next Vote; nor would it do to let himself stand too near the dais, from which central point he might find himself at the tail end of the voting line, should the Proposition Screens begin to glow during the Service. A decisive Vote could be made in ten seconds, but each Kinsman was allowed thirty. The Screen would only propose the bill for five minutes before the Count. That meant that Lloyd must be at least the tenth person in a line in order to be assured his chance to lock his Voteplate in the slot. He'd missed two of his allowable three non-Votes this quarter, already. It would not do to miss another.

THE glow from the dome decreased, suddenly, as the center of the dais unfolded back into fifteen equal wedge-segments, like a blossoming flower, and the Speakster rose into view amid a solemn hush. Bright golden light made the white velvet robe shimmer like a slippery flame, and made the shadowy aspect of the cowl-hidden features all the more terrible. The golden light

From Light-of-Day to Ultra-black, the people of the Hive went about their rigid lives in ignorance of their real ruler, of their true history. How could one slender blonde girl crack this powerful monolithic structure?

spilled upward from the surfaces of the fifteen triangular "petals," bathing the Speakster thoroughly in bright radiance, leaving the remainder of the Temple in even darker darkness by contrast.

The arms of the Speakster rose slowly, angling domeward over his unseen head, until the folds of the weighty sleeves slid back a trifle at the cuff, exposing the wax-white hands, fingers spread wide apart, palms toward the beginning of the dome-curve, as though warding off impending dangers. Lloyd shivered, suddenly, despite the suffocating warmth of the crowd. This would not be a regular Service. That was the Danger stance. Unconsciously, he held his breath, listening, as the mass tension grew unbearably electric.

"There cannot be Service tonight!" thundered the Speakster. "We are polluted from within. It would be sacrilege to have Service with a traitor in our midst." Then, over the rising gasp that arose from the multitude, "She has been traced to this holy place, in a fiendish attempt to lose herself among the masses, to hide her rottenness amid the healthy flesh of the Kinsmen. Remain in your places!" cried the Speakster, as a short-lived Brownian Movement began in the close-packed mob. People froze in place at the peremptory shout. "The Goons have been alerted, and are even now converging through the arcades!" said the Speakster. A sigh of relief whispered like a concerted zephyr over the upturned faces. "She will be found out, have no fear. When I depart, and the Light-of-Day returns, you must exit through the arcade by which you entered. You will be checked

Illustrated by EMSH

THE PROGRAMMED PEOPLE
By JACK SHARKEY

by a squad of Goons on your way out. Remember, a good Kinsman has nothing to fear."

The outstretched arms swung down until the pallid palms came firmly together before the Speakster's chest, the cowled head bowed low, and then the figure on the dais descended from sight, the stiff "petals" re-closing over the spot on which the Speakster had stood, and the golden light vanishing as the Light-of-Day sprang bluely into harsh life against the crystal dome. Lloyd turned obediently, as soon as movement was possible in the dispersing crowd, and started toward his point of entrance, the arcade that would lead him into his sector of the Hive.

Without warning, the Proposition Screens flickered on, and the crowd's movement jerked to a confused halt. Then, as though collectively realizing that there was time enough to be checked by the Goons after the Vote, people formed into neat lines, queuing up before the Vote Boxes that lined the walls.

LLOYD took another look at his watch. Five past eight. That gave him till ten past to arrive at the Vote Box. With mounting anxiety, he counted heads in the line before him. He was twelfth. If each person took the allotted thirty seconds, he'd miss his Vote, have to be hospitalized for Readjustment. He tried to stay calm as the line advanced.

With two minutes to go, he found four people before him. The first, a gray-suited man with very little hair, nocked his plate in the slot—then stood and pondered. It was fully twenty-five seconds before he depressed one of the buttons in the Vote Box's interior, where his choice would remain secret. Another few seconds to retrieve his plate, and then a full six precious seconds while the next person, a skinny woman very near the compulsory retirement age, fumbled in a deep leather purse for her card. And *she* pondered…

Sweat sprang out on Lloyd's forehead. There wouldn't be enough time. There *couldn't* be…unless—

"Miss!" he said, to the back of the small blonde head in front of him. The girl spun about to face him, dark green eyes wide in fright, breath hissing between parted lips. "I didn't mean to startle you," he said, contritely. "It's just that—" It was terrible, telling such an awful confidence to a total stranger, but it was the only way to convince her quickly. "I've missed twice this quarter," he blurted. "Not my fault. I'm a good Kinsman, honestly. It was line-jams, both times. Too many people for too few Vote Boxes. You must believe me."

"What—" she said, a little dazedly. "What can *I* do?"

"Let me have your place in line!" begged Lloyd. "I've timed it. Less than a minute left till Count, and two ahead of me, including yourself. *Please* help me!"

"I—" she said, with a funny, almost hysterical smile. "I don't know why you should be so—" Then she stepped aside, swiftly. "Go ahead. Hurry!"

Lloyd leaped into the breach without even pausing to voice his thanks. As the young man before him stepped away, Lloyd jammed his plate into the slot, and shoved his fingers inside the hand-space. A fumble, and he had a button, he didn't know which one. Pro was right, Con was left, but he just prodded it inward without checking its location. Then the light died on the screen, and his plate popped out of the slot. He caught it deftly, sighed in quavery relief, and turned to thank his benefactor. He saw her, trailing after the departing people toward one of the arcades, shuffling her feet, apparently in no hurry. Then an uncomfortable thought struck him, and he ran to catch up with her.

"Miss!" he said, taking her arm. Again the brief look of fear on her features, then she smiled. It was a small, very tired smile. "You needn't thank me—" she began.

"I wasn't going to—" said Lloyd. Then, embarrassed, "I mean, of *course* I'd thank you, but that isn't why I came after you. I just realized—have *you* missed any Votes this quarter? I'd hate to be the cause of your Readjustment..."

"There's no danger," she said softly, "of my getting in trouble for non-voting."

HE suddenly remembered the words of the Speakster, and dropped the girl's hand as though it had burnt him. "You— you're the—"

"Please!" begged the girl, before his voice could rise in a warning shout to the crowd. "Don't give me away!"

"They'll get you anyhow," he said flatly, with a note of near-pity in his voice. "By rights, I should raise a cry right this instant, to save the Goons the trouble of checking all the good Kinsmen." A secondary thought hit him, and he took a very short step backward. "And you're diseased. The longer you remain in contact with the crowd, the more likely a spread of the contagion."

"I'm *not!*" she almost shouted, then clenched her jaws, and got control of herself. Bright moisture began to trickle from the corners of her eyes, and she dabbed angrily at the warm salty drops. "I was hurt, yes!" she said, suddenly pulling back the long sleeve of her bright green dress, for a brief moment. Lloyd saw the ragged, pink-edged cicatrix on the underside of her forearm, and winced. "It's healed," she said. "I didn't *need* the hospital, don't you see?"

Lloyd saw, and stood there, his mind fumbling dizzily for a direction to take. The last straggling ends of the crowd were moving into the arcades, now. Lloyd took his bearings, saw that only one or two people were now headed for his own arcade, and began to back off in that direction, saying, "I'm sorry, I'm so terribly sorry. I must go, now."

She nodded, once, then turned her back on him, and stood, small and helpless, in the growing void that was the Temple proper. Lloyd turned from her and started toward his arcade. Then he stopped and looked back at her. She was healed, after all. He remembered with a sense of shame the time he'd broken a finger, and hadn't reported for hospital assignment, because a favorite cowboy was at the neighborhood theatre that afternoon. He never *had* gone in, then, being fearful lest the examining doctors notice that he'd delayed. The finger had healed itself, a trifle crookedly, and Lloyd had never told anyone of his dereliction, not even his father. Especially not his father.

Suddenly, he turned and ran back to the girl. "Do they know you?" he said, fiercely, frightened by his own daring.

"Who—who?" gasped the girl, startled by his reappearance. "*Who* know me?" Then, catching his meaning, "The goons, you mean?" Lloyd nodded impatiently. "No, they don't. But they don't have to. I—I have no Voteplate."

"Can't you girls hang onto *anything?*" he muttered. "Don't tell me yours fell in the sea from a Tour-gyro?"

"You say that as though you know somebody whose *did,*" said the girl.

"My fiancée," he explained, adding, with an embarrassed grin, "I'll be twenty-five just after next Marriage Day. I found her in the phonebook listings."

"But— What'd *she* do?" the girl persisted. "Without a Vote-plate, she could be picked up any time, in the first Goon inspection that arose."

"Take this," he urged, pressing something into her hand. "Your arcade is third over from mine. When you get outside, wait. I'll meet you there and get this back. Don't fail me, please."

He spun about and dashed toward his arcade, leaving her standing in the center of the floor, staring dumbfounded at the flat metal plate in her hand. Trembling, she turned toward the indicated arch, and followed swiftly after the stragglers entering it, her perspiring fingers clamped rigidly upon the engraved face of the Voteplate.

CHAPTER TWO

LLOYD didn't like Goons. He knew he was supposed to recognize in them the ultimate in police efficiency, but they still gave him chills. A Goon, a Governmental Opposer of Neutrality, was a fearful sight. All were of a size, equal to a micrometer-breadth, a monstrous eight feet of thick metal and ponderous wheels, bathed from base to apex in the blurry gray pulsations of their protective force fields, through which no power on Earth could penetrate. The metal arms were multi-jointed and dexterous to a fantastic degree, despite the clumsy look of the thick tripodal fingers at the ends of the arms. The "eyes" were wide-set tele-lenses, a pair of them, to report back all they saw to the Brain itself, deep beneath the teeming streets of the Hive. And each Goon spoke with the cold, inflectionless tones of the Brain, the flatly indifferent voice that could only emanate from a mind of glowing vacuum tubes and magnetic fields. From any or all of a Goon's six fingertips could spring the dreaded Snapper Beam, an electronic refinement of vibrations that struck the human nervous system almost identically with the chemical effect of strychnine poisoning, except that a Snapper Beam worked instantly, and always fatally. A brush of the invisible force, and a man's face creased into the frenzied grin of a madman, his legs danced wildly, un-controllably, and the muscles of his back contracted tightly, re-lentlessly, remorselessly, until his spine cracked in two.

Lloyd had never seen it employed, save in the theatres. Dis-persal of insurrection by Goons was a popular theme in films. A mob could be efficiently halted by a sweeping Snapper Beam, to fall like broken puppets. Goons never lost a film battle. Or a real one.

"Name," said the Goon, as the woman in front of Lloyd moved quickly out of the arcade. Goons could not inflect. You had to sense their questions.

"Lloyd Bodger, Junior," said Lloyd, extending his Voteplate for perusal. The three fingers took the plate from his fingers, and slid it into a slot in the chest. A sharp click, and the plate was returned to him, his number now on file in the vast memory banks of the Brain.

"Your sector," said the Goon. With his Voteplate date on file, he would be hard put to tell a lie. Any discrepancy in his statements would go hard on him. He hoped, shakily, that the unknown girl had a sharp memory. She'd only have a few moments to memorize the information on the plate.

These thoughts flickered through Lloyd's mind in the split second between the Goon's second query and his outwardly calm response, "Hundred-Level, Angle One, Unit B."

Lloyd's sector was only one short of being the most important in the Hive. The President lived in Unit A, in the same Angle. Lloyd Bodger, Senior, was Secondary Speakster of the entire Hive. But Goons were no respecters of persons. And less so were they respecters of mere offspring of persons.

"Assignment," droned the Goon.

"Null," said Lloyd, indicating the question was inapplicable.

"Goal," the Goon sub-questioned.

"Secondary Speakster of the Hive by inheritance."

The Goon's arms suddenly dropped to its thick sides, it swiveled completely about-face, and rolled swiftly off toward the far end of the arcade. The interview was over, and it had gone, abruptly as that. There was no "Thanks for your time and trouble," or "You pass inspection," or "That will be all." Goons were built for basic efficiency, not for the subtler nuances of civilized conversation.

OUTSIDE the mouth of the arcade, Light-of-Day was still stark bright blue throughout the Hive. Light-of-Day was dimmed to Ultrablack at ten P.M. every night of the nine-day week save Temple Day, when it was left on until eleven-fifteen, giving time enough for the Kinsmen at the ten P.M. service to return to their sectors. No one went out in Ultrablack. You could see nothing when Light-of-Day went out. A struck flame would burn in Ultrablack, but the light of the flame would not show. Only the Goons could see what went on, then. If going out during Ultrablack were absolutely necessary, as it sometimes was on the Governmental level, a Goon would come and take you to your destination. Being found upon the street after Ultrablack was a form of rebellion; you would then have to be hospitalized for Readjustment.

Just as this last thought was flitting across his mind, Lloyd saw the girl, standing uncertainly at the entrance to the arcade he'd sent her to, a solemn, green-clad figure in the midst of the converging people moving into the entrance toward the nine P.M. service. Her face lighted up when she saw him, and Lloyd was disconcerted to note the tears that sprang to her eyes despite her welcoming smile. "How can I ever—?" she started, but a quick squeeze of his fingers on her arm stopped her.

"Not here," said Lloyd, awkwardly. "Come with me." She fell into step alongside him without question. He led the way to a bar near the inter-level lift. They said nothing to one another until they were seated in a secluded booth, and had pressed the drink-selector that would light alongside their booth number behind the bar. They almost spoke, then, but the waiter showed up too quickly, and they had to wait until he'd checked their ages on the Voteplates and left.

"Why did you do it?" she said softly.

Lloyd made a grimace. "Because I'm a damned fool, I guess."

The girl nodded seriously. You are, you know. Taking a risk like that…you might have been detected, yourself."

Lloyd looked at her, puzzled. "Detected?"

"As a member of the movement, of course," she said. "You're the first I've been able to contact since my escape. The progress you've all made amazes me. Where in heaven did you people learn to duplicate Voteplates? I couldn't believe it when the Goon passed me."

"Hold on—" said Lloyd, pressing his hand furiously hard upon hers where it lay on the smooth tabletop between them. "Don't say anymore, please. You've made an error. I am not a member of your movement." The girl's eyes widened in sudden fear.

"But— Why did you help me? Who are you?"

Lloyd sighed. "I've already answered your first question. And it is with the most abject embarrassment that I answer your second: I'm Lloyd Bodger, the Junior version, the only child of the Secondary Speakster of the Hive." He saw the utter dismay in her face, and added dryly, "Are you impressed?"

"Shattered is more like it," she said when she'd found her voice again. "But an extra Voteplate—"

"I can explain the plate," said Lloyd, "my fiancée, Grace Horton. I was going to her place tonight, after Service, with it."

"But you said she'd dropped it— Oh…I see."

"Exactly. Lost in the sea, from a Tour-gyro. The Goon in the 'gyro saw it happen, which was lucky for Grace. He relayed it instantly to the Brain, and when the 'gyro landed, another Goon was waiting at the field with a temporary pass for her. Another person, by the way, would have needed Readjustment, being so careless, but Grace, as my fiancée, carries just enough weight to get her over the humps. New Voteplates have to be approved through the President's office, of course. When this one came in, today, it was turned over to my father, who gave it to me. I'm not as official as the Goon who'd ordinarily deliver one of these, but even protocol bows to sentiment, now and then."

HE suddenly curled the fingers of the hand beneath his own until they lay fisted in his palm. She looked up at him, then, sensing almost to the word what he was about to say. "Miss— You know I could turn you in for what you inadvertently told me, just now. I won't, though. You have enough counter-information on me to make things hot even for the son of an official."

"I wouldn't—"

"Be that as it may," said Lloyd, "let me say something: Quit. Quit now. Get out of this movement, whatever it is. You can't win, you know. The Goons are invincible. And I hate to think of you, falling under a Snapper Beam."

"Death is death," the girl sighed. "One way or another."

He looked at her, genuinely at sea. "I'm afraid I don't know what you mean, Miss. I only helped you avoid hospitalization because I myself— Well, let my reasons go. But you shouldn't

15

fear going. Sure, it's annoying to be laid up for awhile, out of the swing of things, but—"

The girl pulled her hand away. "You're joking," she said. "You must be joking. If you're truly the son of the Secondary Speakster, you *must* know the truth!"

"I still don't follow you," Lloyd said sincerely.

"You *don't* know!" the girl said, shaken. "You're really convinced that— Listen to me, listen carefully: There are no hospitals! There is no Readjustment! There is only death."

"You're out of your mind," Lloyd said, recoiling from her vehemence. "Of course there are hospitals. I've *seen* them—!"

"Sure," said the girl. "From a Tour-gyro. Or in the movies. But have you ever *been* to one? Have you ever met anybody who *returned* from one?"

"My dear girl," Lloyd protested, really growing concerned for her, "do you realize the odds against meeting a hospital patient? With disease almost completely obliterated, and a civilization of ten million people—!"

"Exactly," said the girl, with a peculiar note of triumph. "Ten million people. Never so much more as ten million and one, and seldom any less. Doesn't that perturb you?"

"The wars—" Lloyd began.

"Please," the girl groaned, shaking her head. "Spare me the enlistment speeches. I know the tales of all the men lost in the battles every quarter, giving their lives in defense of the Hive. Except that there aren't any wars, nor battles, any more! There's nothing out on the planet except wild animals and growing plants. We're the only ten million people on Earth!"

"That's impossible," said Lloyd. "It's childish to be so insular-minded. Our Hive is one of ten thousand such—"

"Have you seen another, even one other?"

"For what?" said Lloyd. "All the Hives are alike."

"They've really got you brainwashed, haven't they? You believe everything the Brain dictates, without question."

"I have to," said Lloyd, with what he thought was irrefutable logic. "There's no way of checking things like— Well, like your story of no wars. I mean, can I be expected to check out ten million people to see if the number of war dead coincides with the total in the Brain?"

"No," said the girl. "You can't. Not so long as your movements are restricted to certain sectors, and you're told which street to use, which side of the street, which direction to walk, which hand to turn the knob with, which—"

"Those are only traffic rules," Lloyd objected. "Can you imagine ten million people all going to the same sector at the same time? It'd be disastrous."

"Sure," said the girl. "For the Brain. People might confer."

LLOYD shrugged and gave up. "I can see there's no dissuading you," he said regretfully. "I only hope that when you're finally caught—"

"They teach me the error of my ways?" she smiled tightly.

"I don't mean it with the inflection you give it," he said. "I really would like to see you get help. You need help, you know."

"The kind I need is the kind you gave me in The Temple," she said. "Illegal help. Shelter. Time to make plans. Time to figure out some way of telling the Hive what's happening to it."

"You know I've gone farther than I should, already."

"I know," she said. She took the Voteplate from her handbag, and held it musingly in her fingers. "I really should keep this," she said, then saw the sudden anxiety in his eyes and relented. "Here, take it." She slid it under his hand. Lloyd palmed it gratefully. "Our movement could use a hammerlock on a higher-up," she said, almost wistfully. "But you're too nice a guy to put the screws on. It'd be a cruel way to show my gratitude for what you did tonight."

"I did nothing, really," Lloyd said. "I simply saw how fearful you were of the hospital, and didn't have the heart to turn you in."

"Wait," said the girl. Lloyd stopped speaking. She looked thoughtful, then leaned forward, very confidentially, and asked,

"Does your father like you? Do you two get along?"

"What is this?" Lloyd demanded suspiciously. "Instant psychoanalysis?"

"Nothing like that," the girl snapped, exasperated. "I mean, does he *like* you, as a son, care what *happens* to you?"

"Well," Lloyd said, slowly, "he'd probably beat my head in for what I pulled, tonight, with you...but...yes, he does like me. And he cares about my welfare."

"Then do this one favor for me," said the girl. "When you get to your Unit tonight, tell him you feel rotten, all sick inside, and that you think you should be hospitalized."

"But why should I——?"

"Just tell him. And make it convincing. And, if he really cares about you— See what happens." She rose from her place. "It'll look funny if I leave alone. Walk me to the street?"

Once outside, she glanced about, uneasily. "It's after ten. Got to find a place to hide before Ultrablack."

"But listen——" Lloyd said, abruptly realizing the grim night that lay in store for her, with blinding blackness like a palpable pall in the streets, and only Goons rolling through the empty streets. "You've got to have *someplace* to go."

"Is there someplace? Without a Voteplate?" she said with weary rhetoric. "I think not. Thanks. Goodnight. And goodbye."

SHE started off down the street. Lloyd hesitated a moment then rushed after her. "Wait, I'll hide you."

"Why should you take such a risk, for me?" she said.

"It's not for you," Lloyd said, telling as the full truth something that was only part of the whole. "It's for me. Purely selfish. I risk more if you're caught tonight. When they question you, under truth drugs, about your escape from the Temple and I'm sure *that* has them curious. You will be unable to avoid implicating me."

"Is—is that your only reason? Your own skin?" she said.

"Yes," he said, forcing conviction into the word.

She shrugged and took his arm. "A fugitive can't afford to be choosy. I have no prospect of escape but you. I'll let you hide me…if it'll make you feel safer."

Lloyd nodded, and started toward the lift that would take the two of them up to the Hundred-Level. It was only as they got aboard, and he'd keyed the lift switch with his Voteplate, that he thought to ask, "By the way—what's your name?"

"Andra," she said. "Andra Corby."

"A nice name. I like it," said Lloyd. "I wasn't sure if you'd tell me your name."

Andra shrugged. "It'll be in tomorrow's papers, anyway."

Lloyd looked at her uncomfortably, but she was staring straight ahead at the grillwork gate of the lift.

CHAPTER THREE

GRACE HORTON appraised herself in the mirror, and was not pleased with what she saw. "Face it, Grace," she said aloud. "You are positively hopeless." She tilted her head to one side. "Well, nearly hopeless." Her eyes were good, that was something. Wide, gray and thickly lashed, they were her best feature. Her nose was just too snub to be pert. Her mouth, though her lips were generous, and her teeth well aligned, had too much slack at the outer edges. She either held it in a perpetual smile, "An easy way to be mistaken for an idiot," she remarked bitterly—or it sagged. Her hair, an unfortunate mustard-and--brass shade, would not hold a curl for more than two hours at the outside. "All I need," she decided ruefully, "is a brand-new head."

Grace leaned away from the mirror to consult the alarm clock that lay almost hidden behind an impressive array of cosmetics. Five till eleven. "He's not coming," she said to her image. "Give it up girl. He said he'd come, and he probably meant it when he said it, but he's not coming." She turned from the mirror and began to undress, beside the single three-quarter-sized bed. "And why should he come?" she asked herself tiredly. "He doesn't love you. He never—to his credit, damn it—said he did, either. Hive Law requires that all males shall marry by the age of twenty-five, or be taken for Readjustment. Bachelors are not good for racial survival, unquote. Unwed girls may list themselves in the classified section of the phone book, along with their qualifications, then start sweating it out by the phone. So I did, so he called me, so we're engaged. But that doesn't mean we have to like it. Or that he has to, anyhow. And I'm not sure that I do."

Grace toyed a moment with the idea of submitting herself for Readjustment, then gave it up. "A new face wouldn't help," she decided. "What I need is a new outlook. Besides, what have I got to crab about? I'm engaged, I'm only twenty-four, and someday I'll be the wife of Secondary Speakster of the Hive. So hurray for me," she added, listlessly, as she flipped the coverlet back, and hopped into bed. She lay there in the glaring Light-of-Day, waiting for Ultrablack. When it came, in a soundless rush of darkness, she spoke just once more. "But why didn't he come?"

CHAPTER FOUR

DIDN'T you tell your future daughter-in-law she'd been reassigned to a new Temple Day? asked the President. "She went last night, regardless."

The man addressed, Lloyd Bodger, Senior, scratched his head. "Seems to me I did, Fred. I could have forgotten, of course."

He nodded and shrugged the topic away. "Probably hated to miss a chance to be with your boy. Nice kid, that Lloyd."

"Thanks," Bodger said dryly, keeping a firm eye on his superior. Stanton was buttering him up to something, he knew. "Full of youthful spirits, too, your boy. I can easily understand why he might—well—grow overly romantic."

"Come to the point, Fred," said Bodger. "Lloyd's behavior can't hurt you unless it hits your only sensitive area: your public image. So what's he done? Drunk too much, pinched a waitress's rump, scratched a four-letter word on a Temple?"

"Don't take this too lightly, fellow Speakster," said Stanton, purposefully. "Running the Hive is like walking on eggs in hot cleats. You're either careful or things get a mite sticky."

"We always have the Goons," said Bodger.

"A Hive full of ten million back-broken corpses isn't much of a domain," snapped the President. "Have you forgotten that extra-marital peccadillos are frowned upon in Hive society? People who play around get hospitalized, quick."

"So what has all this to do with my son?" demanded Bodger.

"He was seen, last night, bringing his fiancée up to this level, shortly before Ultrablack."

Bodger sighed, then nodded slowly and leaned back in his chair. "And the girl?" he said grimly.

"So far as I know, she's still on your premises. I think you had better have a talk with her. And your son."

"I'm sorry, Fred," said Bodger. "I'll make certain there is no recurrence."

"You'd better," said the President. "If I topple, you're on the next pedestal down. I might drag you along, just by inertia." He turned and left the office with cold dignity.

"*Crap!*" the elder Bodger spat aloud. "I've *told* that kid to toe the mark in public!"

CHAPTER FIVE

BODGER had only a short distance to walk to Unit B from his office. His temper, despite his efforts at self-control, was seething dangerously when he entered his foyer. He crossed the mammoth parlor toward the archway at its rear, where a short corridor led to the sleeping quarters. Bodger arrived at the door of his son's bedroom. Then, with his hand upon the knob, he froze, and a ghastly pallor spread itself across his rugged features.

A hand came up swiftly to his stomach, holding it, pressing

inward against the sudden spasm he had felt, and he stepped swiftly across the few remaining feet of carpeted hallway to the door of his own room, through it, and swiftly into his personal bathroom, locking the thick door behind him. The room was swimming like a thing seen through warm oil as he slid open the mirrored panel of the medicine chest and removed a large jar of pale granulated crystals. Violently nauseated, he managed to unscrew the lid and dump a handful of the crystals into the water tumbler. He ran the warm water into the tumbler—it would dissolve the crystals faster—and drank the now-glutinous solution. Then the tumbler fell from his weak, perspiring fingers and smashed into spicules in the basin. He took no notice, hands rigid against the rim of the basin, shoulders shaking uncontrollably, his large, gray-thatched head sunken wearily upon his chest. He stood like that for two minutes, until the room began to settle down, and its outlines took on solidity once more.

"A close one," he muttered, aloud.

When the eyes that met his in the glass were no longer bleared with sick pain, he combed his hair neatly, and impatiently began to remove his sweat-soaked shirt and necktie. Before returning to his bedroom to change into fresh dry garments, he slid the mirrored panel closed. It clicked sharply and locked. Countersunk into the tiled wall, there was no indication that such a space existed behind it. Only Bodger, Senior, knew which tiles to depress in which order to open that panel. In a disease-free society, a medicine chest was taboo; it implied that its user had no faith in the Government-run hospitals. Bodger went into his bedroom, dropping the damp shirt and tie atop the clothes hamper in the closet. There was an ancient leather bag, with shoulder strap, on the closet floor. Bodger carried this out into the room, opened the flap.

When a small light glowed on the indicator panel, he lifted a short metal rod, and played the end of it slowly back and forth just below his fleshy ribs. The light flickered on and off steadily. Bodger looked sharply at the needle of a dial beside the light.

"Thank heaven," he whispered, and returned case and contents to the closet. Then, after laying out a set of dry things, he considered a moment, ran a hand testily over his stomach region, and grunted in annoyance. He was still slightly overwrought; he could feel the juices inside him itching to spurt into his bloodstream and arouse him into his erstwhile pitch of anger. It wouldn't do. It wouldn't do at all.

Angered at his own infirmity, he nevertheless set the alarm for an hour's time ahead, in case he dozed, then lay back on the bed and closed his eyes.

IN the adjoining room, where the door to the hallway was securely bolted, Lloyd Bodger, Junior, stood up near the wall, in a stance he'd held for many minutes, the side of his head pressed tightly against the plastic paneling. "I think he's lying down," he whispered. "I heard the bedsprings creak."

Andra Corby, her face lowered against the knees which she hugged to her chest on the bed, shivered a bit, then straightened her long, smooth legs until she was simply pillow-propped against the headboard once more, and her arms had refolded across her breast. "Are you sure?" she asked tautly. "The longer I stay here, the more frightened I become."

Lloyd spun to face her, almost angrily. "Will you stop that relentless nobility! I'm doing this for my own skin, remember? I don't care what happens to you; I care what happens to me if something happens to you!"

"Your father," she said, enunciating with icy calm and slow clarity, "is going to *hear* you."

Lloyd controlled himself, his fists knotting at his sides.

Seeing he was relaxing, Andra said, a little less frigidly, "I thought...I thought he was coming in *here.*"

"He stopped outside my door, all right..." Lloyd mused. "Then went to his room in a rush. I don't get it."

He listened some more at the wall. Behind him, Andra giggled, suddenly. He glanced at her. "What—?"

"I just thought— What if your father's on the other side,

listening to hear what *you're* doing. I'm just picturing two grown men, frowning in earnest concentration, their ears separated by a few inches of plastic, and it's funny."

"Not if you're correct, it isn't," said Lloyd, and Andra stopped smiling. "As soon as he hears you, the jig's up."

"Maybe—" She leaned forward with eager hope. "Maybe it would be a good thing, Lloyd. He's a powerful man in the Hive. If he knew your problem, he could use his influence to do something, couldn't he?"

"My father loves me, sure," said Lloyd, with a wry quirk to his lips. "But I don't think he loves anything so much as his position in our society. My consorting with a fugitive might put the kibosh on the next election."

Just then the phone rang and Lloyd couldn't avoid knocking Andra to the floor in his effort to get the receiver off the hook before the bell could shatter the silence once more.

"Hello?" he said, extending an upright palm toward Andra to beg her continued silence.

"Lloyd?" said a subdued, tense female voice.

"Grace," he said, remembering his promise to come by with her card. "What—what do you want?"

"I've got to see you, Lloyd," she said. "About last night."

"When?" he asked.

"As soon as you can make it."

"Well—Maybe in…" Lloyd peered across the room at his bureau clock. Almost noon. Nonessential lift usage precluded until after the twelve-to-one lunch period. If he hurried, he could key the lift-switch before the ban. Lifts in use were never disempowered. "If I catch the lift, fifteen minutes. Otherwise not till after one."

"…All right."

LLOYD grabbed his jacket from the back of a chair. Andra stood up, apparently unharmed, and slid into her shoes. "Where are we going?" she asked, smoothing her dress.

Lloyd looked at her. He hadn't considered—"I guess you'd

better come with me," he said. "I'd hate you caught in the house. In my bedroom especially."

There were seconds to spare when he closed the gate and thumbed Grace's level, the ninety-third. Anyone was permitted to travel to a level beneath their own. To go higher, you needed a duly authorized Voteplate, or an invitation from a higher-level dweller. The lift dropped smoothly down inside the shaft. Halfway to Grace's level, a red light glowed on the level-indicator. When they reached their getting-off place, the buttons would function no more until one o'clock. It saved needless crowding if lunching workers remained on their own levels. Otherwise, if a line were too long, a worker might be tempted to try his luck lower down, and if too many decided simultaneously, the bland flow of human traffic might be imbalanced, agglomerated beyond the capacity of the transportation systems. Inefficiency would result, with people returning late to their work, restaurants having too much leftover food, or not enough to go around. The Hive was too delicately geared for imbalance. So the lifts went off during lunch.

"Grace Horton must be trusted," Andra said suddenly. "Look, Lloyd," she clutched his arm, forcing him to meet her gaze and listen. "If she hasn't found out, fine. Even Goons can't find out what a person doesn't know. But if she has found out someone else used her cards—and called you, instead of reporting it to the authorities. Then she can be trusted to hear about me."

"I hope you're right," said Lloyd. The gate opened.

"We'll never find out standing here," said Andra, "Come on, Lloyd." She started out ahead of him. He pondered the courage of this small blonde girl, then felt a wave of shame at his own cowardice. He was in this up to his earlobes already. No amount of explaining could ever make up his hours of ignoring the basic laws of the Hive. And he simultaneously realized two things: If Andra's theories were all wrong, he would merely be Readjusted and returned to his life same as before. And if they were correct—what difference did it make how long he dallied with the Hive's opposition? You could only be destroyed once, and even his delay in shouting the alarm when he'd recognized Andra as the fugitive was grounds for a medical checkup.

"What the hell," Lloyd said miserably to himself. He was no safer standing on the cross-sector walk than in the depths of dark intrigue with Andra.

CHAPTER SIX

"BODGER!...*Bodger!*"

A hand was shaking his shoulder roughly, the elder Bodger realized with annoyance. His eyes focused on the face of Fredric Stanton. Bodger shrugged the hand away, and sat up groggily.

"As I always suspected," he said, brushing at the crusted salt on his chest, "the Hive can't run an hour without me at the helm." He got to his feet and stretched.

Stanton, frowning at his sarcasm, let it pass without comment; he had a more important topic to discuss. "The tally of last evening's Vote just came in to my office," he said tightly. "It was a near-complete poll, only a few thousand missing."

Bodger, still trying to get his mind readjusted to the idea of being wide awake again, started toward the bathroom and a warm shower, muttering, "Hooray for progress. Is that any reason to waken a man—"

"*Bodger—*"

He stopped at the open door to the bathroom and turned his head toward the President. "All right, out with it." Without knowing how, exactly, Bodger knew it was about Lloyd again. And worse than before.

Stanton reached inside his suit jacket and withdrew a folded legal paper, a black-lettered stiff document with an illuminated margin of pale orange. "I have here," he said, watching Bodger's face, "an order for Readjustment. It just came up the tube from the Brain. Do I have to read you the name of the Kinsman on it?"

"Good lord," Bodger whispered. "What—what could he possibly have done to—"

"As I said, there was a Vote last night. The proposition was a simple one: "Shall, in the interests of good government, the draft age be lowered to fifteen?" You want to know how Lloyd voted?"

"Not *con!?* He has more brains than to— I've told him all the catch phrases that demand a *pro* Vote. Is there any possibility of...?"

"Error?" Stanton smiled bitterly. "You of all people should know better. It was Lloyd's plate in the slot when the Vote was cast all right. The Brain can't be wrong on that. The alternative solutions to the problem-alternatives to his making a deliberate Vote against the interests of good government, I mean—are very few: One...he was not paying attention to the screen. Two...he struck the can button by accident. Three...he let somebody else use his plate. Anyone of which reasons is in itself grounds for Readjustment!"

"Fred, you wouldn't...."

"Of course not, Bodger. I had the incident erased from the memory circuits immediately. This is the only copy of his Readjustment order. You can keep it, tear it up...frame it, if you like! That's not why I'm here."

"You don't have to tell me," Bodger sighed. "In the past sixteen hours, the son of the Secondary Speakster has blithely violated the social and political ethics of the Hive, to the extent that his destruction—"

"Bodger!" Stanton flared. "You have a rotten habit of—"

"Pretty words don't alleviate the truth of the situation. You know, and *I* know, what Readjustment is! A one-way trip down the incinerator chute!"

"All right, we know it! So shut up about it, and let's keep it to ourselves! What I'm here to find out is...what the hell are you going to do about this idiot son of yours? This is twice he's had to be covered for, in a damned short time, Bodger. I can't spend my time rescuing Lloyd from something I'm starting to think he may well deserve!"

"Aw, Fred, you wouldn't let—"

"The hell I wouldn't! I like Lloyd, and I like you, but if it starts shaking up my position in the Hive, the two of you can go to blazes! Do I make myself clear?"

"I—I'll talk to him, Fred, really I will."

"You mean you *haven't?*" Stanton exploded. "What's the idea of coming home here in the middle of the day, then? I thought you were going to—" He took a closer look at the other man, then scowled. "Say, are you all right, Bodger? Your color's kind of funny. You're not...sick?"

"Of course not!" Bodger snapped. "I'm shaken, if you must know. I came right home here to chew Lloyd out for last night's episode with the Horton girl, and when I couldn't find him, I got so mad that I thought I'd better lie down and cool off. I don't want a scene if I meet him in a public place. *That would* get the word out in a hurry, wouldn't it!"

"Still, you look kind of—" Stanton halted, and gave the subject up with a sigh. "Maybe I'd be, too...if I got a couple of jolts like you did. Okay, Bodger. See you back at the office, later." He turned and went out.

BODGER stood listening until heard the front door close. Then, still shirtless, he went into the hallway and threw open the door of Lloyd's room without knocking. It was empty. But there was the elusive memory of a sweet fragrance still hovering in the air there. Bodger swore softly, and returned to his own room to shower and dress. He had some heavy thinking to do.

When, minutes later, he was refreshed, dressed, and ready to appear in public again, he'd made a decision. He needed to discover the root of Lloyd's dangerous behavior. And the likely person to know something about it would be Lloyd's fiancée, Grace Horton.

Bodger left his Unit and started toward the lift. It was still short of one o'clock, but the Voteplate of the Secondary

Speakster cut through a lot of mechanical red tape.

The lift arrived at Hundred-Level within seconds after his nocking his plate beside the call-button. He got aboard and began the descent toward Ninety-Three.

CHAPTER SEVEN

ROBERT LENNICK leaned far back in his swivel chair, and sighed a deep sigh at the ceiling, being careful it would not be heard by the party on the ether end of the wire.

"Now, listen, sweetheart," he said. "You are good. Got that? Good, with a capital tremendous. But you don't click in urban dramas. You're too…" he didn't want to say tall, or gigantic, though these words were more readily at tongue-tip, "…too Junoesque for the parts we're casting…no, I mean it. You just…well, you're just not the housewife *type,* darling!"

The speaker crackled in his ear for another minute, and Lennick sat and studied the piled-up scripts in his in-box with wearily narrowed eyes. When his chance came again, he said, "No, not today. I'm sorry, Lona, really I am…it's impossible, that's why. All right, if you have to know…we're shooting Frederic Stanton, that's why—"

The speaker's reply to the phrase made some of the color wash out of Lennick's smooth shaven face, and this time he interrupted with a snarl. "You better watch it, Lona, baby! A smart aleck pun like that can get you sent to the hospital. You know damned well I mean we're going to photograph him…okay, but simmer down, huh!? Okay, baby, I will…yes, as soon as *anything,* anything at *all* in your line comes by my desk…word of honor…sure thing…yeah, that'd be lovely. We'll do it sometime…okay, Lona…Lona…I said…o-*kay,* Lona!" He spat out the last words, and clamped the phone into the cradle with vicious pleasure. "Dumb broad!" he mumbled, then got up and opened the door to his anteroom.

"Sorry to keep you waiting, Frank," he said to the tall, gangly youth who rose from a chrome-and-plastic chair and came into the main office.

The man called Frank sank into a chair and fiddled idly with a button on his shirt until Lennick had the door closed again. When the youthful producer was once more back in his swivel chair, eyeing his visitor, Frank lost his casual air and locked eyes with him, disconcertingly steady blue eyes, and Lennick had to fight an impulse to wince.

"Trouble?" he said, after a moment.

Frank knitted his brows, and cupped his upper lip in the moist curve of his lower before replying, without emotion, "Depends." He fiddled with the button again, then gave it up and stood. He preferred pacing as he talked. "It's...well, it's about Andra, Bob."

Lennick stiffened. "They got her...?" His relief was only a conditional relaxation when the other man shook his head; he was keyed to tighten up again without notice. "So where is she? How is she?"

"Fine, to answer your second question. I don't know the answer to the first, though I could make some guesses. The thing is...we better get the word out to the others not to try and contact her."

"*Not to—!?*" said Lennick, stunned. "But she needs help, bad. She has to hide until we can—!...Frank, what's the matter? You look so damned funny!"

"Okay, I'll level with you, Bob." Frank stood at the front of the desk and leaned his hands on the blotter, staring down at the anxious face of his friend. "Last night, after her escape, Andra tried to hide in the Temple, up on ninety-five. The Goons were right after her, Bob. There wasn't even any Service because of her. Every person in that Temple was checked—*one* by *one*—for Voteplates. She *had* one, Bob. She got *out.*"

"That's crazy!" Lennick gasped. "Where in hell? Frank, I saw them collect her Voteplate after the accident. She couldn't have gotten it back. And she couldn't have a spare, I know, so—?" He saw the uneasiness still in the man Frank's features, and was quiet. "There's more?"

"After her escape," Frank said flatly, taking no joy in telling the tale, "She met a man, outside the arcade, went with him for cocktails, then up to his level. That's the last she was seen, Bob. It was the Hundred-Level. None of us are authorized to go that high without escort."

"But who the hell did Andra know on the top?" Bob blurted.

"She's given autographs to a few higher-ups. But—"

"It was Lloyd Bodger, Junior, Bob. They acted like old friends. Now do you see why I think it's unwise if she's contacted?"

LENNICK suddenly surged from his chair and nearly tore the shirtfront from his visitor in an angry fist, as he yanked the other's face close to his own. "You can't mean that about Andra, Frank. You know her! You've worked with her. And I—I know her better than anyone, Frank. She's not a traitor. She wouldn't betray us."

"I wish," said Frank, calmly ignoring the enraged aspect of Lennick's attitude, "you'd put your heart back where it belongs and think it over just once with your brains…"

Bright beads of moisture suddenly appeared in Lennick's eyes, and he released his grasp of the other man's shirt and sank down into his chair, burying his face upon his arms. "There's an explanation," he mumbled into the blotter. "I know there is. She wouldn't—" he lifted his head, suddenly hopeful. "Frank, we're still here! If she told all she knew, we'd be atomized by now, right?'

Frank looked uncertain. "Maybe. At least…it's a point in her favor. I don't know. You've got me shook, now." He sat back down and pondered, shaking his head slowly back and forth. "If she isn't hollering for the Goons— What's she doing with Junior? A guy like that doesn't take perfect strangers up to his place, does he?"

"I don't believe that part at all," said Lennick. "She may've gotten off before he did."

"The indicator went right on up without stopping. My witness'll swear to it. Right to top level, just before Ultrablack."

"Maybe she's under arrest, going for questioning," Lennick parried weakly. "It could be, you know."

"Why up there? Goons carry Truth Serum. Besides, the witness further states that they didn't look like anything but a couple of chummy dates. Real chummy."

"How about if— Maybe he was helping her? Andra's not a bad looker—if she turned on the tears—"

"You've been reading your own scripts, friend," said Frank, not unkindly. "This is reality we're dealing with, not never-never-land on film. This Lloyd Bodger, Junior is not the boy--most-likely when it comes to helping anti-Hive people. Face it, Bob. Something's up."

"So why, I repeat, aren't we all on our way down the chute costumes, cameras and all?"

"That's the only thing that doesn't make sense," Frank admitted. "And the only thing that prevents me hiring a sniper to knock her off."

"You'd do that?" said Bob. "To Andra?"

"For the time being, we'll let it ride," Frank decided on the doorstep. "It may be handing ourselves over on a silver salver, but...we'll let it ride. Till we hear from her. And she'd better make it convincing."

"I know she'd tell me the truth...whatever it is," said Bob, then regretted his rhetorical lapse into doubt. But Frank let it pass, and simply said, with a fleeting smile of compassion, "If I were you, I'd take that Goon's advice, from yesterday when Andra was carted off: Get engaged to somebody else."

"I want to talk to her," Bob insisted.

"If it was your neck, fine. Talk. But it's all our necks. I can't risk it."

"You could fix it, Frank. You could find out where she is, a way to get there. Come along, even, so I don't fumble the ball. Please, Frank? I've got to know..."

"Bob, if you knew what you were asking!" Then the taut, painful set of his friend's features cracked away some of his veneer, and he slumped wearily against the jamb, fiddling with that button again. "So maybe insanity's catching, or something," he said after a pause.

"You'll help me?"

"I'm not absolutely sure I can, Bob. But...tell you what...Buzz me about nine tonight. I might have an idea."

"Thanks," Bob said. "You're—you're a nice guy, Frank."

Frank turned and walked across the anteroom and out, without replying. Robert Lennick settled back in the swivel chair again, this time not at all relaxed.

CHAPTER EIGHT

NOW, in this scene, sir, you're instructing the Temples through the Speaksters, in your capacity as Prime Speakster," Robert Lennick was explaining, as Frederic Stanton nodded over the pages of script.

Frank, the director, stood by impatiently while his boss explained the setup of the scene they were to shoot.

"I think I understand," Stanton said finally. "Where do I go, now?" An aide led the President toward the waiting set. When he was out of earshot, Frank inclined his head toward Lennick, and whispered, "Never mind buzzing me tonight, Bob. Meet me here, at your office, just before Ultrablack."

"Before Ultrablack!?" Lennick said, aghast. "How will we—?"

"Leave it to me, okay!" said Frank, impatiently. "I'll get you to Andra, wherever she is. I want to see her myself."

Lennick could only stand stupefied as the tall, angular form of the director moved off toward the waiting cameras and crew. Then he grunted in frustration and turned back toward his office. The presence of Stanton made his mind return to the day before, when Andra was captured by the Goons, and it bothered him to dwell on it. An accident. A stupid accident on the set. She'd entered to do her scene, had caught her foot on a hidden guy-wire, and had fallen, still holding the tray of drinks she'd been supposed to serve to her co-stars. And the ragged edge of a shattered goblet had raked across her forearm. Not deep, not at all. Just a long, blood-oozing scratch. The Goons had been there almost on the instant, commandeering her Voteplate, taking her off for "treatment." And she'd looked to him for help, help he could not give, dared not give. And when she saw she was suddenly friendless, she'd broken and run. The Goons hadn't expected such a reaction. Before they could relay the situation to the Brain and get their instructions, Andra had dodged out by a corridor too narrow for them to follow, in all their ponderous girth and height, and had vanished completely. Later that day, a Goon Squad had come to the studio and widened the corridor, and one other like it, to preclude such a thing ever occurring again.

Lennick was worried at Andra's not contacting him. She might think he couldn't be trusted, the way he'd let the Goons take her. But what did she expect a man to do against armed Goons? She'd only have had the dubious pleasure of seeing him dance to death with a hideous smile on his face, while a Snapper Beam broke his spine in two.

It made Lennick's head hurt to think about it, so when he got to his office, he started reading some new scripts. In a society where the possession of medicine is a crime, it didn't pay to have a headache. Or to let on you had one. But he couldn't erase the look he'd seen in her eyes when they were taking her away.

CHAPTER NINE

ARRIVING at the door to Grace Horton's Unit, Lloyd paused with his finger not quite pressing the bell. "This won't be pleasant," he warned. "I've never done anything like this before—getting involved with you, I mean—and I don't think Grace is going to like it. I can't much blame her, either."

He stopped as the door opened. Grace Horton stood there, clad only in a fragile garment of light silk, her upturned face warm and eager. Beyond her, Lloyd saw the tray with a bottle, ice, and two glasses. There was soft music playing from somewhere in the Unit. He felt his face go red.

"Grace…I want you to meet Andra, Andra Corby."

Grace looked past him for the first time, and saw the other woman. A tiny spasmodic reaction tightened her face and some of the color drained away. Then she said, with rigid composure, "Come in. Come in, won't you?" Unconsciously, she held the folds of her garment tightly at the throat with one hand, as if to make her covering more substantial, as she stepped aside to let them pass.

"Excuse me," she blurted suddenly, after shutting the door, and rushed into her bedroom. The music emanating from there cut off, abruptly, and then Grace reappeared in the doorway, her lips curled in a smile that would not quite come off. "I thought——I thought you'd miss the lift," she said, in an obvious extemporization that was embarrassing to all three persons. "That's why I'm—not quite dressed, yet. I thought I'd be ready after one, when you—" Her eyes fell on the tray, with its solitary preparation for two, and her voice choked off in the middle of a syllable.

Then she took a breath, walked into the parlor, and sat down gracefully on the arm of the sofa. "Well," she said brightly, "now what'll we lie about? "

"I'm so very sorry, Grace," Lloyd said contritely. "I…I would've told you Andra was coming, if I'd known. We only decided after I'd hung up—"

Grace's eyebrows rose just a fraction. "Andra was at your home when I called?" She rose, suddenly. "I think I'd better get another glass from the kitchen. I have the feeling we're all of us going to need strength."

Lloyd and Andra looked at one another, then sat gloomily down in armchairs deliberately far apart, and waited for Grace's return. When she came back with the third glass, she was a bit more composed.

"Now," said Grace, after draining half her glass, "we can

talk."

There was a silence, then Lloyd broke it, awkwardly, with, "You said you wanted to see me here—right away."

"I called you about the Temple Service last night, Lloyd. I see by your face that you do know something about it. Good. Maybe you can tell me what— Don't look so shaken."

"I...okay...you caught me off-balance, I guess."

"I must have. You look like you were just kicked in the stomach. Well, then, tell me: What happened last night?"

"How did you know anything happened?" Lloyd asked.

"A call from the top level this morning. I was warned not to attend on the wrong night in the future, and told I was being let off the hook—though they phrased it more politely, of course— because I was engaged to the son of the Secondary Speakster."

"Did you—? What did you say? To their call?" Lloyd asked, knotting up inside.

Grace folded her arms and leaned back. "I'm no dope, Lloyd. I knew you had my Voteplate, and were bringing it to me last night. That is..." she interjected with chagrin,"...I thought you'd be over last night with it. When you didn't come, and I got this call, from top level, I kind of figured you were in dutch, somehow, and played along. I apologized for my error, and promised it wouldn't happen again. I see, by the way you two just let your breaths out, that I did the right thing...or did I? I take it Andra was the one who used my plate?" Lloyd nodded, miserably.

GRACE thought this over, watching the two of them, then leaned forward and touched Lloyd's fingers where they curled tightly around the end of the chair arm. "Apparently, I have salvaged everybody's chestnuts. Would it be asking too much if I wondered what the hell my reasons were?"

"I'll explain," Lloyd said. "That is, as best I can. My motivations are still a bit obscure even to myself."

Grace flicked a glance at Andra, sitting small and lovely and feminine in the chair. "Are they!" she said, a spark of intuition putting her almost with complete accuracy ahead of Lloyd's still-untold tale. "Maybe I can figure them out for you after I hear your story, then."

"Okay, Grace," Lloyd said gratefully, missing her inflection. He proceeded to tell her the story, from the time he'd gone to the Temple up until the present moment, eliding only the fact that Andra had spent the night in his room. He used the phrase "up at my Unit" and hoped it wouldn't be proved any deeper than that. When he'd finished, Grace looked dazed.

"You mean...you *believe* all that, Lloyd?" she said. "I used to have great respect for your sanity, but...this thing about no hospitals, about bumping off the Kinsmen to keep the population level down...It's crazy, Lloyd. Look, your father's one jump from the Presidency. Has he ever, in all the years of your life, even *hinted* such a thing to you?"

"No, of course not, but—"

"Yet you take the word of a fugitive, an obvious mental case who doesn't know what's good for her—"

"May *I* say something in my defense!?" Andra protested.

"You may not," said Grace, then turned back to Lloyd as though Andra had ceased to exist anymore. "How could a man with your intelligence—"

"Hold it!" Lloyd snapped. "Hold it right there. I'm not a complete fool, Grace. Sure I had doubts. But there are some things Andra said that bother me. And I thought up a few puzzlers myself. Like war. Casualties in battle account for a high rate of the deaths reported in the Hive, right? So it occurred to me...how come we're not using the *Goons* to fight in the war? They're indestructible, they're armed with our most potent weapons...yet we let men and boys be shipped out of here to fight. It doesn't make sense."

"Of course it does!" Grace retorted. "You think that question never occurred to anyone but you, Lloyd Bodger? We don't use Goons in war for the same reason they didn't use atomic weapons after the Second World War of last century: The *other* side has them, and might fight back with them."

"But—so what!" Lloyd exploded. "What's the difference if our people are killed by other soldier's bullets or by enemy Goons?"

"There's—here's less slaughter this way," Grace said, with an intensity that sounded lame even to her.

"All right, we'll let that part go," Lloyd said, in no mental shape for argument. "There are other things—"

"Forget them," Grace said, vehemently. "Whatever your reasons, or reasoning, last night, you have another problem to face: What are you going to do with this girl? The longer you stick with her, the slimmer your excuses will sound when she's caught. In fact, the only hope you have is to turn her in, right now, and pray your Readjustment isn't too painful."

"But don't you see; Grace—" Lloyd blurted. "*What if she's right?* On that chance, no matter how silly you think her theory is—a theory that has led others to join her movement, remember—do I dare take the *risk* of turning her in?"

Grace stared at him and digested this aspect of the situation slowly. "I—I guess it would be kind of late, when the top level sent me the report that your Readjustment hadn't taken, or something, to say 'Well, he told me so!'"

The door chimes pealed, then, startling them all.

"You expecting anyone else?" asked Lloyd.

"No, unless your friend the fugitive was seen coming in here."

As they spoke, Andra had gone to a window and peeked out from behind the curtain. When she turned to face them again, her face was gray with strain and apprehension.

"Lloyd—" she said. "It's your...father!"

CHAPTER TEN

UNDER the blazing arc lights on the set, President Stanton played himself to the hilt, nearing the climactic, "Vote for the sake of the Kinsmen! Vote for the freedom of the Temples! Vote for the life of the Hive!" Just as he launched into this most important part of the script, a page boy made his labyrinthine way on tiptoe through the cables and reflectors and sound equipment to the chair of the director, and whispered urgently in his ear. Frank got to his feet immediately.

"Cut!" he called.

Stanton looked up in some surprise, and it was a very baffled cameraman who finally found enough strength to cut off his machine. The set was dead quiet as Stanton arose from behind the prop-desk and looked in unpleasant speculation at the source of the interruption.

Frank cleared his throat, and said, "I'm sorry. The scene was going well, sir; that isn't why I cut it. You have a phone call, in Mr. Lennick's office."

"I thought it was understood I was not to be disturbed while on the set," said Stanton, still wondering if he should give vent to his feelings of outrage.

"It was, sir. And is. But the call's from your personal secretary, sir. She says it's of the utmost importance."

Stanton hesitated, dropped his script back down onto the desk, then started decisively around the side of the desk toward the director. "She had better be correct," he said darkly, brushing by Frank and the crewmen without apology and vanishing into the corridor that led to Robert Lennick's office. There was a brief silence, then a concerted sigh of relief from the men on the set.

"Shall we wait," one of the crewmen asked Frank, "or shoot around this scene and pick it up later?"

Frank spread his hands. "I don't *know*. I have to be sure he's coming back, first—I'll go find out." He told his staff to relax until his return, then hurried out after the President.

A hundred feet down the corridor, he rounded a turn. Up ahead he saw Stanton just entering Lennick's office. Then, without hesitation, Frank ducked into a nearby office, his own, and locked the door on the inside. The lowest drawer of his desk had a false bottom. He triggered the release on this, now, and lifted out the small black earphone-set there, setting it dexterously across his head, magnetic speaker directly over his ear. In the hollow of the now-exposed section was a telephone dial. Frank swiftly spun it through the sequence of Lennick's office number, then sat hunched forward over his desk, listening hard. He heard Stanton pick up the phone, and say, "This is Stanton. What is it?"

Madge Benedict, his personal secretary, "It's Lloyd Bodger, Junior. You told me to contact you the instant he got out of line again. Well, he has, but good."

"As bad as the other two?" Stanton queried.

"Worse, much worse, sir. Bad enough to make the other two look good by comparison. He was seen, this afternoon, on Ninety-Three-Level, in the company of Andra Corby, the fugitive from hospitalization. You know, sir, the movie star who was injured on the set yesterday."

Something sparked in Stanton's brain, then, and a hard light of comprehension dawned in his eyes. "Wait...let me think...of course. She vanished yesterday from the Temple on Ninety-Five! And Lloyd was there, too. I wonder—" He stopped idle speculation and snapped, "Get me Bodger, quick!"

"His office," Madge told him after a moment on another line, "says he's gone home, and you can—"

"I *know* he's at home." Stanton growled, "I just left him there. Get him!"

There was a short silence, then she spoke again. "I'm ringing him, sir. I don't think he's at home. No one answers."

"You know what to do as well as I do," he said impatiently. "Put a tracer on his Voteplate. See where he's gone to."

Another pause, while Madge coded an inquiry and flashed it to the memory circuits of the enormous Brain beneath the Hive, and received the near-instantaneous reply. "Sir," she replied, "he's taken the lift to Ninety-Three-Level. The same place his son was seen."

"That's odd...do you suppose he knows about the Corby girl, too? Or—" Stanton dropped the interrogation; Madge shouldn't be made to think about it. The less she knew, trusted secretary or not, the better. "Skip it," he said abruptly. "Find out for me where they might be going on that level, their hangouts, haunts, and friends..."

Madge found the answers and got back on the line. "Three possible places, sir. Dewey's Bar and Grill, in Sector Three, Miss Grace Horton's Unit, and—"

"Lloyd's fiancée?" Stanton interjected. "The one who attended the wrong Temple Service last night..."

"I believe she did, sir. We sent out a memo—"

"And she got it this morning. Of course!" said Stanton, exultantly. "And phoned Lloyd right afterwards!"

"I don't follow you, sir—" Madge said, blankly.

"Forget it," snapped the President. "I have all the information I need. And," he added, with belated gratitude, "thank you for calling me, Miss Benedict." He hung up without waiting for her reply.

Huddled over the desk in the dimness of his own office, Frank tore off the earphones, dropped them back into the hollow of the drawer, and re-closed the false bottom. He was out in the corridor again, headed toward Lennick's office, with seconds to spare when Stanton came out.

"Sir," Frank said, turning about and falling into step with him on the way back to the set, "I wonder if you'd care to finish the scene, or should we shoot around it?"

"Shoot around it," Stanton said. "I can't be bothered with the filming, today. Something's come up."

Frank nodded and let his pace slacken, allowing the President to move away from him. After poising on his toes for an undecided second, he whirled and dashed toward Lennick's office. If young Bodger had been seen with Andra, in the same locale where the elder Bodger was now heading— or had even arrived—there was going to be an explosion. An explosion that might sweep Andra, the Bodgers, and the entire anti-Hive movement with it, when Stanton got the wheels of his office in motion.

CHAPTER ELEVEN

AFTER thumbing the doorbell the second time, Bodger shifted his hand toward the inner pocket where he kept his Voteplate. The doors of all Units in the Hive were keyed by the Voteplate of the dweller, through a slot above the knob. As Secondary Speakster, Bodger's plate could key any door in the Hive save Stanton's; all doors opened to the President's Voteplate. Just as his fingers touched the edge of the plate in his pocket, he saw the knob start to turn, and withdrew his hand. The door opened, and his son was standing there.

"Come in, Dad," Lloyd said, standing aside. "Grace will join us in a moment."

The elder Bodger's eyes did not miss the fact that the door to the bedroom was closed, as he entered the parlor. This delayed appearance of Grace, coupled with the delay in their response to his ring, confirmed his worst suspicions. He took the seat Lloyd offered him, leaned back without quite relaxing, and came to the point at once.

"Lloyd, you're making trouble. Lots of it. For yourself, and quite possibly for me, too. I don't like it. But before I take any steps, I want to hear your side of it."

Lloyd sat down facing his father, very uncomfortable inside. He didn't want to inadvertently volunteer more information than his father already had. He could think of plenty of things he'd done since the night before, any one of which was damnable; the safest policy was in determining just what, and how much of what, his father knew.

"I'm not sure I follow you, Dad," he said, pleasantly. "What kind of trouble—"

"Don't fence with *me*, young man," said his father. "Unless you're completely brainless, you know what I—" He was about to expostulate on the disgraceful conduct of the evening before, the matter of Grace's having gone up to top level with his son, then decided to let that ride until Grace herself was present.

Keeping steely control over his emotions, he said, instead, "The Vote last night, Lloyd. Your plate was credited with a con Vote. Are you insane, Lloyd? Haven't I told you—"

Lloyd racked his brain to recall the content of the proposition, but could not. "Maybe I hit the wrong button," he said lamely. "My hand might have slipped."

"The penalty's the same, whatever the basis of your stupid action, and you know it!" his father rasped. "I don't think you are even able to tell me what the proposition *was*, are you!" A look at Lloyd's burning face told him the answer. "I thought not," he said, wearily. "I don't know what I'm going to do with you, son. I've tried to keep you in line—"

The entrance of Grace Horton stopped Bodger's tired lament, and both men rose to their feet.

"It's nice to see you Mr. Bodger. Would—would you like a drink?" Grace offered, nervously.

"I would not—" he said, then softened his curt reply with, "But thank you, anyway, Grace. Maybe later, after I've had my say." Lloyd and Grace looked at one another in numb apprehension of the unknown, then back at Bodger.

"The son of a prominent man," Bodger began, at last finding his approach-path, "has a great responsibility to his father's good name. The Hive, as you both know, has rigid rules regarding...well...amorous conduct, to employ a euphemism, between unmarried persons. Yet, last night, Lloyd...Grace...the two of you were seen going to top level on the public lift, just before Ultrablack."

A SHORT sound from Grace's chair was the gasp that had sucked itself between her lips as the significance of Bodger's words reached her.

Lloyd, for his part, fought but could not control the hot crimson flood that rushed into his features when he met Grace's hurt gaze.

Bodger, misinterpreting both their reactions according to his own notion of the night before, immediately said, "No need to be afraid. A thing like this is better out in the open. I can understand how two young people in love might—"

"*Dad!*" Lloyd said abruptly. Bodger halted and waited for his son's words. Lloyd, speaking to his father the words that were actually intended for Grace's ears, said, with deep earnest, "It wasn't like that, Dad. She slept on my bed, with her clothes on. I slept on the rug. We—we just had to be together, that's all. I've done nothing you should feel ashamed of."

The sudden smile on Grace's face caught at Lloyd's heart.

"That's a help, son," Bodger said, likewise convinced. "To me, at any rate. The point, unfortunately, is that any persons who observed you going up to our Unit with Grace could not be expected to presume the best, if you see what I mean?"

"I do, Dad," Lloyd mumbled contritely. "And I wish it had never happened."

"It wouldn't have," Bodger pontificated, "if Grace hadn't gone to the wrong Temple Service. I can see how she might dislike the change in her attendance-period, meaning she'd be unable to attend with you, anymore, but it was the wrong thing to do. If she'd stayed home, none of this would've happened."

The irony of this last statement, while it missed Bodger completely, brought a small, one-syllable burst of laughter from Grace's lips, which she quickly stopped. Lloyd jumped into the breach swiftly, to distract his father from a dangerous line of conjecture.

"Dad, there was something bothered me last night…in the Temple, I mean, about that fugitive girl?"

"What about her?" said his father, unprepared for the statement to the extent that he made an automatic response without having time to notice he was being diverted.

"The check-up for the girl, Dad. It seemed kind of…I hate to use the word…*inefficient*…at least to me."

"The girl had no Voteplate," Bodger said, puzzled. "I should think a check of all Voteplates was efficient enough."

"But why not have the Goons check her description, or her

fingerprints, or even check for the scar on her arm?" said Lloyd. "It'd be much simpler, and surer."

Bodger shook his head. "Not at all, Lloyd. A Goon, you must remember, doesn't 'see' as we do. Its television lenses are only geared to recognize streets, Units, sectors, and so on, and to tell Goons from Kinsmen. Anything as delicate as actual recognition of a face would involve the building of a Brain greater in mass than the current one. No. Voteplates were the only answer to identification problems; that's half the reason they exist. As to fingerprints...they will serve in identifying an individual, it's true, if a person's identity is in doubt. But it takes time, and the fingerprint files are enormous; to do so in trying to locate one person in a full Temple gathering would have taken many hours, and there was a time element involved. The ensuing Service could not begin until the Temple was emptied. Finally, as to the scar..." Bodger looked decidedly uncomfortable, then sighed and said, "As son of the Secondary Speakster-and-future-daughter-in-law, Grace, perhaps it's time you were told a fact that is rather embarrassing to the regime, but all too true: In the Hive, people do not always report injuries. While we do not enjoy this mild form of treason to the planned medical facilities of the Hive, we nevertheless tolerate it, for the simple reason that it's bothersome treating every scratch and bruise that occurs, most of which will heal themselves. And so, if we had the Goons check for the girl's scar, we might have found a large number of medical violations among the Kinsmen at the Service. Under that circumstance, we would have to hospitalize everyone; Goons are trained to spot any deviation from a healthy norm beyond a certain degree. It would have been terribly awkward, all around. So the only sure method was—"

BODGER stopped, as though violently stunned. "Lloyd—" Bodger said, his heart hammering with a nameless dread. "*I* was activating the Temple Speaksters last night. I gave the warning about the girl to your Temple. I remember distinctly what I said. And I know I made no mention of the type or location of her injury. No mention at all. *How did you know it?"*

Lloyd's lips worked, but he couldn't bring up a syllable from his constricting lungs. Grace her hands knotted into fists, looked at the carpet, and sat like a marble statue.

Bodger got to his feet, towering over the two of them.

"I'm talking to you, Lloyd. Answer me! How did you know!"

Lloyd's ribs abruptly began to function again, and he drew in what felt like the deepest breath of his life. Then he stood and faced his father, defiantly.

"Because she's here, Dad. Right behind that door. And Andra Corby was the girl in our Unit last night, furthermore. I helped her escape from the Temple, with Grace's Voteplate. Now, what are you going to do about it?"

Bodger fell back into his chair like a crumpling jointed doll, his face shocked and incredulous. "I don't believe it," he said stiffly, pressing his hands upon the chair arms to halt their trembling. "Lloyd, it's not true!"

The bedroom door opened, then, and Andra came out. When Bodger saw her, something inside him cracked, and he suddenly dropped his face into his hands and just groaned. Lloyd was at his side in an instant.

"Dad," he said, gripping the other man's shoulders, "Dad I had to tell you. I've been entangling myself in so many lies since last night...it was the only thing left to do!"

Bodger looked up, wide-eyed with dismay, and shrugged Lloyd's hands away. "Let me think," he said, hoarsely. "I have to think. Stanton mustn't find this out. I've already covered up for your idiotic Vote, and for your taking Grace—all right, Andra—up to our Unit last night. There has to be a way to prevent your horrible errors being found out. I'll cover, somehow, Lloyd. If I can find a way, I'll cover up, and—"

"Dad—!"

Something in the young man's tone made Bodger stop his frantic raving. He looked into his son's eyes, and saw the question even before Lloyd asked it.

"Why should you cover up?"

Bodger grabbed at his shattered self-control, and sat up, stiffly. "I—I don't follow you, son."

"I said," Lloyd repeated sadly, "why should you cover up for me? I'll only be hospitalized for Readjustment, won't I?...*won't I?*"

"Lloyd," Bodger said sickly, getting up and clutching his son's hands, "you're overwrought, right now, you've been under a strain..."

"All the more reason for my hospitalization, then," Lloyd said, with all the relentless cruelty he could muster in the face of his father's ghastly fright.

"No!" Bodger yelled. "You can't go! You don't understand, Lloyd! I can't explain here."

"There's no need to," Lloyd said, suddenly softening and taking his father by the hands to halt their frenetic quavering. "Your attitude has told me all I want to know. Andra was speaking the truth. There are no hospitals, no treatment, no Readjustment. Only death."

"Lloyd—!" Bodger said. "If you only knew why—"

"We'd all like to know why," said Andra, solicitously. "Mr. Bodger, it's no use struggling any more. You have to tell the truth, now, or have your son...along with Grace and myself...destroyed."

"All right," Bodger said. "I will. I'll tell you the whys and wherefores of the Hive. Then maybe you'll—"

"I'm afraid such an extemporaneous educational program is quite impossible," came a voice from the doorway.

FREDRIC STANTON, just removing his Voteplate from the slot in Grace's door, had his other hand extended toward them. And clutched firmly in his steady grasp was the stubby metal muzzle of a Snapper.

The two men and women stepped backward, slowly, as he advanced into the parlor and shut the door behind him. "I only heard the last few phrases of your conversation, unfortunately," he said. "I think, for the interests of the Hive, that I should hear it all. We'll have to go up to my office, all of us, to get at the truth. I'll have a Goon Squad pick us up, here." He reached for the phone, dialed swiftly, and soon had Madge on the line. He kept the Snapper trained on the group while he spoke, and never took his eyes off them.

"Sir," Madge replied, before he could ring off, "do you think it's wise, bringing Bodger through the streets under guard, I mean?" She sounded greatly concerned. "The Kinsmen—"

Stanton narrowed his eyes appreciatively, and cut her off with, "You're right, of course; it wouldn't do to let public opinion of the regime get any shakier than it is. I can't wait till Ultrablack, however. Start the emergency sirens at once. Allow fifteen minutes for all Kinsmen to clear the streets. Then put on the Emergency Ultrablack."

"Right, sir," Madge said, and hung up.

Stanton smiled, still keeping them covered as he replaced the phone in the cradle. "You'd better be seated," he said congenially.

CHAPTER TWELVE

YOU really believe that Bodger is involved in the anti-Hive movement?" Lennick said dubiously. "It doesn't make sense, Frank. Why should the Secondary—"

"All I know," Frank said determinedly, "is that Stanton was shaken by the news of young Bodger and Andra. It puts me right back on Andra's team, all at once. If Stanton was in the dark, then it's very doubtful that Andra's done anything to betray the movement; the greater likelihood is that she's pulled Junior our way."

Lennick frowned doubtfully. "Andra's an attractive girl, Frank, but—"

"Everybody isn't pulled into the movement like you were, Bob. Sex appeal has its uses, but there's also a thing known as intelligence. Bodger and his son are no dopes. If she convinced them—"

"Why *should* she?" Lennick said angrily. "Have to convince them, I mean! Didn't they, of all people, *know?*"

Frank stood there with his mouth open, blinking. Then he sat down and stared at the producer, dazed. "I must be getting soft-headed," he murmured after a short hiatus. "Of course they must know. Still—?" He looked helplessly to Lennick for assistance.

"I know; it doesn't make sense," Lennick nodded. "The only thing to be done is to find Andra, I guess, and ask her the answers. Conjecture is only taking us in circles."

Frank spoke tautly, his pent-up frustration making his words strained and painful. "Excepting that, as long as Andra's in Grace Horton's sector, we can't go after her. That's not one of the permitted areas on my Voteplate. I'd hate to be caught loitering in that area when the Goons show up for Andra. When they make an arrest, they check on everybody. If only this had occurred later, today, near Ultrablack—"

"Why do you keep stressing Ultrablack?" Lennick asked. "I still haven't even figured out why I was to meet you here tonight just before it was turned on. We'd really be helpless then."

"Bob," Frank said gently, "this is nothing personal, but-…well when the movement gets a new member, we don't just lay out all our schemes on a red carpet for him. There's a trial period for all new members. You've been on probation for a couple of months, now. The less you know of our plans, our memberships, the less you could spill if you were a plant."

Lennick grinned wryly and shook his head. "I know. That was a real bone of contention between Andra and myself when we'd been engaged nearly six weeks. A wife can't keep secret meetings from her husband very well; he may suspect her outings are something even worse. When I finally pressed her about broken dates, and times she couldn't be reached, and she told me about the movement, I was pretty miffed she didn't trust me with all she knew."

"She couldn't, Bob, you know that. The information wasn't

hers to give out, without permission of the rest of us. We could not put our necks in a noose because Andra adores your big brown eyes."

"I'm surprised you're still speaking to me, after yesterday," Lennick said with chagrin.

"Bob, you did what any of us could have done: Nothing. One man can't fight off a Goon Squad. We would have lost two members, instead of just Andra, if you'd put up a fuss."

"But about Ultrablack," Bob said, frowning. "I know you people have meetings after Light-of-Day goes off. *How* you do it is beyond me, with the streets alive with Goons, and darkness everywhere, even indoors."

IF there were a chance of rescuing Andra when tonight's Ultrablack came on, I'd tell you, Bob," Frank said sincerely. "It'd give you the chance you didn't have yesterday to do something for her. I think you can be trusted. I trusted you enough, just now, to tell you about the tapped phone."

"You had to," Lennick said with a shrug. "Or else I'd be leery about believing you knew so much about Stanton's private call."

"We set that up ever since Stanton started appearing in our Hive-located scripts. He's always so busy, keeping in touch with his office between takes, that we've kept one jump ahead of the Goons, on occasion. It must drive him nuts, wondering about the raids that never came off."

Lennick got to his feet. "I wish we didn't have to just sit here this way. At this very moment, Andra may be still uncaptured. If she could be warned—"

"She could, if top-level privilege didn't entitle young Bodger's fiancée to an unlisted number. You can go up there if you want, but—I know too much about the movement to risk it. If you're caught, it's unimportant—insofar as the sum of your knowledge, I mean. But I don't dare let myself be taken."

Frank paused, and cocked his head, listening. Lennick, seeing him, did the same. A keening wail penetrated into the depths of the office. "Sirens!" Frank said. "It means there'll be an emergency Ultra-black in fifteen minutes. Or even less, if we did not hear them from the very beginning…"

"You think it has to do with Andra?" asked Lennick.

"No telling," said Frank. "And no telling how long this Ultrablack is for. At normal Ultrablack, I can count on a definite number of hours, but—" He hesitated, then clapped Lennick on the shoulder and said, "Come on, Bob! This may be the chance we were looking for!"

The producer followed him, bewildered, out of the office and down the corridor toward the set. Just inside the set, where the siren-alerted crewmembers were grabbing their gear together in preparation for swift flight, Frank pulled Bob aside and led him to a door flanking the corridor entrance. "This way," he said, shoving the other man inside and following.

"To the prop room?" Lennick said wonderingly, his mind a pastiche of envisioned secret panels, inter-level tunnels and the like. Frank kept moving down the short hall without replying, so Lennick could only tag impatiently after him, his curiosity at its ultimate. Then they were in the high, barn-like gloom of the prop room, a fantastic collage of canvas backdrops, teeter-piled furniture, swords, pistols, fake-currency stacks, ropes, saddles, bows, arrows, and other oddments of the trade.

LENNICK found his bewilderment growing as Frank pushed aside a stack of dusty chairs and then slid aside a tall desert-sky backdrop on oiled rollers. For a horrible instant, Lennick recoiled, his flesh going icy with unthinking fright. Then he relaxed and gave a shiver of relief. "Damn those things!" he grunted. "I forgot we had them stored back here…" Then he looked up and met Frank's gaze, and comprehension dawned on him. "You mean…*them!?*"

"There's a panel in the back, where the operator can slide in to run the controls," Frank said. "It'll hold two, if you don't mind crowding."

"Good grief!" Lennick gasped. "I should have guessed."

"Never mind the self-recriminations," Frank said. "Help me roll this thing out so we can get inside it."

Lennick nodded, and took hold of the jointed metal arm on one side, as Frank did the same on the other. Together, they wheeled the massive torso of the prop-Goon toward the center of the room. As Frank located and opened the neatly disguised panel, Lennick shook his head in doubt.

"There's no force-field, Frank," he said uneasily, "and once Ultrablack sets in—"

"Unlatch the door to the street," Frank said testily, "and stop asking so many questions." As Lennick hurried to comply, Frank added, with less irritation, "The absent forcefield's the reason we use Goons only after Ultrablack. A Goon won't notice the difference, since it only determines identities by shape, but a Kinsman would, instantly, as you just did. There are no Kinsmen out after Ultrablack, so that's the safe time for us. As for your other worry, about how we'll see after Ultrablack, Ultra-black is only the jamming of the visible spectrum by the radiation of inverted light; the compression and rarefaction phases of the light waves are plugged, dovetailed into, by the opposing phases of inverted light. Goons," he said, depressing a switch beside a small cathode-screen inside the hollow body, "see by cutting off the sensitivity of their lenses to light or inverted light, it doesn't matter which. Then the hive is bright as daylight to them."

Lennick clambered up beside him and helped Frank dog the metal panel shut. Side by side, hunched over the pale blue glow of the screen, they watched the interior of the prop room through the lens-eyes of their grotesque conveyance. When the sirens halted, Ultra-black swept the room from their eyes like a velvet curtain. Then Frank turned a dial, and the room re-appeared on the screen, like a negative image, with white for black, and vice versa.

"Now we can go," Frank said, releasing a brake. The prop-Goon began to roll ponderously toward the door to the street, carrying its two perspiring conspirators. "I only wish," Frank said tensely, guiding their movement out into the Kinsmen-deserted street of the sector, "that this thing had Snapper-beams, too. But I guess an underground movement can't have everything."

CHAPTER THIRTEEN

THE four prisoners sat glumly looking at the impenetrable squares of darkness outside Grace Horton's windows, awaiting the arrival of the Goon Squad. Madge Benedict, without needing to be told, had kept Ultrablack from occurring in the Unit; it was the only area of visible light in the entire nine cubic miles of the Hive. Stanton, his weapon never wavering, lolled against the wall of Grace's parlor, watching their discomfiture with amusement. Of the entire group, Andra's pallor was the worst, and Stanton noted this fact with relish.

"I don't expect to glean much from the minds of the others," he said, addressing her directly, "but yours must be a veritable treasure trove of interesting data."

"I don't know why you should think so," Andra said, knowing all the while that fabrication was futile; five minutes under truth serum would prove the President's contention beyond debate. "I'm only one small cog in a wheel greater than your whole Goondom of force."

"You almost convince me," Stanton said. "But…no matter. I'll know the truth in a few more minutes."

"And then what?" asked Grace. "What happens to us once you've picked our brains of knowledge? If it's death—"

"Grace—" Lloyd said warningly, taking her arm. She turned on him.

"Darling, if we're to die in any event, let's die now. At least we'll have the satisfaction that a hundred other people aren't dying afterward, because of us."

"She's right, Fred," Bodger said, smiling for the first time since his arrival at Grace's Unit. "If you kill us now, you'll never find anything out. At least our lives will have accomplished something, if only continued secrecy about the movement."

"A Snapper Beam needn't kill, if used briefly enough," Stanton said mildly. "If you four prefer dancing an agonized quadrille until the arrival of the squad, you have only to come an inch closer. In fact, unless you return to your chairs at once, I may just do it anyhow, for my own diversion."

"A Snapper Beam," said Bodger, "is effective only so long as it's held upon its victim. Can you play yours four ways at once, Fred? Because, while you're gunning anyone of us down, three will be diving for your throat!"

STANTON, before Bodger's statement could bring the others in a unified wave against him, pointed the muzzle of the Snapper directly at the man's chest and pressed the firing stud. A whine of power came from the weapon as the invisible forces lashed out.

And Bodger took two strides forward and smashed his fist into Stanton's face. The President's head snapped back with the unexpected blow, and cracked sharply against the wall. Then, the weapon falling from his limp fingers, he slid to the floor and collapsed in an untidy heap.

Bodger, stumbling back from the fallen body, sagged into a chair, gasping. Lloyd sprang to his side, dropped to one knee beside the chair, staring in unbelief at the shaken man. "Dad!" he blurted, in dazed joy. "You're alive! You're all right!"

"No…" Bodger said, his eyes bulging as he shook his head, his lips thickening over words that were becoming difficult to formulate. "No, Lloyd. I'm sicker than I thought."

"What are you talking about, Dad? You just took a dose of power that would've destroyed a healthy human nervous system, and came through it. How can you say—"

"Lloyd!" Bodger rasped, clutching his son's arm. "Don't you see? I don't—don't have a human nervous system, anymore. The thing I've always feared has happened. I—" He coughed, and his skin took on a sickly bluish tinge for a moment, then flushed into a ruddier tone as he took a breath and held himself in rigid control. "The—the Brain. You…must go to the Brain, Lloyd. I—can't talk more. Ask it, why is the Hive…" His voice trailed off, and his eyes closed.

"Dad," Lloyd said, shaking his rather by the shoulders. "Why is the Hive *what?* Tell me!"

His father opened his eyes and stared unseeing beyond his son. His lips, flecked with spume, worked silently, then he gurgled, "M—medicine…bathroom…behind mirror…I n—need—" His collapse this time was total, his head hanging limply with chin on chest, his arms sliding over the sides of the chair until his wrists touched the carpet.

A thunderous pounding upon the front door brought Lloyd and the two women up short, and they stood frozen with dread as the insistent sound continued. The inner surface of the door was shaking with the blows. "Goons?" whimpered Grace. "What'll we do if it's the Goons?"

"Stanton's Voteplate!" Andra snapped. "Lloyd, take it, quick, out of his pocket!" Lloyd caught her meaning instantly, and hurried to obey. "Grace, count ten, then open the door. We can't delay longer than that. Lloyd, think fast, and think smart! We're all in your hands, now!"

Lloyd, the plate in his hand, shoved his own into Stanton's pocket and straightened up. "Let them in, Grace," he commanded. "Then both of you keep still and let me talk."

GRACE unbolted the door and stepped back. The six metal bodies of the Goon Squad rumbled loudly as they crossed over the sill and came to a halt before the trio. The Goon in the forefront of the group, swiveling its glittering tele-lenses over them, spoke in its cold, emotionless voice, "President Stanton."

Lloyd stepped forward and handed over the Voteplate. The eight-foot metal creature took it, slipped it into its chest slot and paused; then returned the plate.

"Correct," it said. "Orders."

"Miss Madge Benedict, of my office, to be taken into custody at once, and held incommunicado," said Lloyd, figuring Stanton would be helpless with no contact at top level, so long as Ultrablack prevented his leaving the unit.

The Goon stood silently as this information was relayed to the Brain and thence to the Goon Squad nearest Stanton's office. "Accomplished," it said flatly, after a minute, its dull gray force field pulsating with incredible energies. "Orders."

"Secondary Speakster Bodger—the man in the chair—to be taken," Lloyd flashed a glance at Grace, who nodded, "along with this woman on my right, to his Unit on Hundred-Level, Unit B, and left there without supervision, by all but one of your squad."

"Orders."

"One of you will escort me and this woman on my left to the Brain, in Sub-Level Three, immediately."

"Orders."

"All orders conveyed," said Lloyd.

CHAPTER FOURTEEN

KNOWING only the sector in which Andra had been seen with Lloyd, but not having access to Grace's address or phone number, Lennick and Frank, in the prop-Goon, arrived at her Unit many minutes after the Goon Squad had left. They found it by the simple expedient of noting—in their white-for-black cathode screen—the one Unit from whose windows blackness was trying to pour. That meant Light-of-Day was still functioning in that particular Unit, and that in turn meant only the presence of higher-ups.

The door to the Unit lay wide open, but Frank didn't dare roll inside. His conveyance's lack of a force field would be readily apparent in such close quarters. He halted, instead, a few yards along the side of the Unit, told Bob where the door lay from them, then cut off his motor and the cathode screen. Ultrablack fell about them like a velvet wall.

Bob, following Frank, felt his way out into the near-palpable darkness, found the wall against his fingers, and edged along beside it, fingers feeling for the doorway. A hand upon his chest stopped him, and he waited.

Frank, holding Bob back, leaned carefully toward the open doorway his fingers had just touched, not daring to show any more of himself than he had to whomever might be inside the Unit. Then, swiftly, he leaned his head out of Ultrablack and blinked at the parlor before him. He saw no one. He closed his fingers upon the front of Bob's shirt, gave a quick tug on it, then let go and stepped into the room. A moment later, Bob was there beside him, squinting against the bright bluish Light-of-Day.

"Maybe it's the wrong Unit," Bob offered. "A malfunction in the Hive mechanism *might* keep this place from Ultra—" He shut up and gripped Frank's arm. "Stanton," he said, pointing beyond the sofa. Then Frank saw the President. Cautiously, the two men approached the still, silent figure and stared down at him.

"What do you suppose happened?" Bob said, shakily. "Do you think Andra had something to do with this?"

Frank Shawn scratched his head. "You got me. All I can figure is—if Stanton's in a fix like this—he may not have been able to get her picked up. This tableau has the earmarks of turned tables, if you ask me."

"Do we dare waken him and find out?" Bob said, keeping his voice to a library-whisper.

"Not as long as Ultrablack's on. We'd have a hell of a time explaining how we got here," said Frank, shaking his head. He turned to look at Stanton again, and the blood froze in his veins. Stanton's eyes were open, and he was staring at the two of them with glaring hate.

"How did you get here, Kinsman Shawn?" he demanded. "And you, Kinsman Lennick!" Stanton lifted his head from the floor, awkwardly, and tried to look around. "Bodger! Where is he?" he said, shaken by a sudden return of memory.

"I've got to get to that phone! They're probably on their way to my office right this minute. If they take control—" He choked on the word and lay still, seeing the Snapper—his own—that Frank now leveled at him. "I suppose the two of you know this is high treason?" he said wearily. He lay there fuming at his enforced impotence.

Bob looked at Frank. "What'll we do?"

"I wish I knew." Frank muttered. "If we knew what had happened, where the others have gone— But we don't, so there's no follow-up there...still, we can't leave Stanton here, now that he's seen us, or it's our necks when he gets free."

"We..." Bob said, hesitantly. "We could make sure he would not be able to do anything, later..." He let his voice trail off, Frank caught his meaning after an instant's puzzled frown, and went ashen.

"In cold blood, just like that?" he said softly.

"I don't like it any more than you, Frank, but—" Bob spread his hands helplessly. "What choice do we have? If we're caught—you especially—the whole movement is doomed." He stood silent, waiting for his answer.

Frank nodded, abruptly. "You're right. It has to be done." Stanton looked from the face of one man to the other, his tongue licking suddenly dry lips.

"Bob— Frank—" Stanton spoke from the floor, his tone weak with dread. "You wouldn't kill me, I'm an old man. You wouldn't kill me, would you? I'll do any thing. Forget I've seen you here, even...anything...only please don't!"

LISTEN, Frank," Bob said, trembling. "You heard what Stanton said: They've gone to his office. Take the Goon and go after them. I'll stay here with Stanton. If everything works out about the revolt...fine. If it doesn't— Call me, here. The number's on the phone base. If the balloon goes up...I'll kill Stanton, then. But unless it does...I can't..."

"Okay," Frank said, coming to a swift decision. He noted Grace's number, then went toward the Ultrablack beyond the door. At the threshold, he turned. "I may not get the chance to phone," he said. "If things go wrong, I mean. Give me half an hour. If I haven't called by then—" He avoided looking at Stanton's perspiring face. "Go ahead."

Bob reached out and took the Snapper. "Good luck," he said. Frank nodded wordlessly, and stepped out into the blackness. In another minute, Bob heard the rumble of the prop-Goon's motors, and then the whir of its wheels on the pavement outside. When it died in the distance, he looked down at his prisoner.

"I'm sorry, sir," he said, "really sorry. It was the only thing to do, while he was here. I knew he wouldn't go through with it. Killing you, I mean." He stooped and helped him up.

"What if he'd agreed?" Stanton complained, taking his weapon and pocketing it.

Bob looked up, surprised.

"I'd have had to kill him, of course. Without your permission, I didn't dare let on in front of him. I thought you'd want me in a position of trust, still. Frank won't alert any other members of the movement against me, this way."

Stanton grunted noncommittally at the statement, and got to his feet. Then he stepped to the phone and dialed Madge Benedict's number. The receiver shrilled in his ear, over and over, as the phone in her office rang. He waited for six rings, then hung up, his face thoughtful.

"Madge is never supposed to leave the phone without my permission during an emergency. Something's happened. They may be up there already...they must be up there already!"

"What can we do?" Bob blurted, frightened. "Once they gain control of the Speaksters—"

"That takes time," Stanton said. "They'll have to lift Ultrablack, flash an emergency call to the Temples on the Proposition Screens, and wait until the Kinsmen have arrived to make their announcements. But there's a way to stop them. The Goons. And they're controlled by the Brain—or by whomever is at the controls of the Brain," he added with a smile that sent gooseflesh along Lennick's back.

"But how can we get there in Ultrablack?" Bob asked. "If

we wait for them to turn it on, we won't have much time before the Kinsmen get to the Temples..." He stopped when he saw what Stanton was doing. The President, from an inner pocket of his coat, had taken a sort of transparent gray oval of some plastic material, and was fitting it before his eyes by means of an elastic strap. When it was in place, he could just barely see the President's balefully glaring eyes. "I didn't know such a thing existed," he said, knowing what the eye-shield was for, suddenly.

"Few people do," said Stanton. "Come on, you young fool! Take my arm and let's get moving!"

Bob took a firm grip upon the President's sleeve, and then the two of them stepped out into Ultrablack. Despite his youth, Bob had a difficult time keeping up with the other man. Stanton was driven by extremely vengeful fires.

CHAPTER FIFTEEN

THE end of the line for the lift was Sub-Level One, just beneath the granite soil on which the Hive rested. Lloyd and Andra emerged there, keeping close to their towering metal guide. Lloyd had only been to the Brain a few times, with his father. He knew very little about its operation. What he did know would have to suffice.

There was a sharp, hard click, as the Goon between them sprouted neat metal cogs on its wheels. Then, the cogs fitting neatly along tread and riser, it guided them down the steep staircase to Sub-Level Two. This level was smaller than any in the Hive itself. A mere twenty-five feet in height, it was filled completely with concrete and lead, save for the ten-by-ten-foot space to which the stairs had led them. In the center of this space was a circular door, on the floor near their feet. The Goon could come no further.

"Orders," it said dispassionately, after lifting the heavy door with one hand and guiding Lloyd to the brink of the gaping hole with the other.

"Return to your squad, and forget where you have brought us."

"Orders."

"All orders conveyed."

The Goon rattled off into the darkness, and Lloyd heard it begin to ascend the stairs once more. He felt for, and found, Andra's arm, and drew her to him. "Careful, now," he cautioned her. The Brain control chamber is right under us. We have a hundred-foot climb down a steel ladder, now."

"But I can't see—" Andra said, holding back.

"There's Light-of-Day below," Lloyd said. "As soon as we start into the chamber, we'll be able to see. Ultrablack never goes on in the Brain." He held her hand tightly as he felt for the top rung with his toe. "Okay, now, I'm starting down. Come a little closer, and take your weight off one leg. I'll guide that foot to the top rung."

Andra caught herself nodding in the blackness, and said, "All right," aloud. She heard Lloyd's feet clumping onto something that clanged dully, and then his hand was taking her gently by the ankle. She let him place her foot on the rung, then gave him a moment to begin his own descent before she followed after him. Three steps down, and she was in bright Light-of-Day, on a shiny tubular ladder whose base looked impossibly far below her. She shut her eyes and clung tightly to the sides of the ladder, then, taking step by cautious step downwards. The rungs, she'd noted, were just about a foot apart. She'd count to one hundred, and if she hadn't reached the bottom by then, she would scream.

When she was just enumerating ninety-seven, Lloyd's hands took her by the waist, and lifted her to the floor. She opened her eyes, disengaged his hands from her body, and then looked around in awe.

TIER upon tier of lightweight metal scaffolding rose on all sides of a twenty-foot-square area of flooring. Riveted across the angles of the scaffolding were coils and condensers, insulators and sparking forks of synaptic wiring, whirling cams and clattering selectors, banks of glowing lights that danced on random pattern, deep-set labyrinthine nests of wire that glowed a brilliant orange, then faded to dull gray, then glowed again, accompanied by a rising and falling hum of urgent power.

As Andra's eyes followed the amazing array from ceiling to floor, she was shocked to see that the flooring was not really the solid thing she had supposed; it was, rather, a taut network of heavy cable, really nothing more than a glorified window screen, through the interstices of which she caught a vertiginous glimpse of more areas of bright electrical light, dropping away below her feet to incredible distances.

"How big is the Brain?" she said to Lloyd, pulling her eyes from the terror of the empty depths between the frameworks beneath the cable-floor.

"A cubic mile," Lloyd said. "It's self-oiling, self-repairing, self-replacing. And in it are stored all the memories of the Hive from the day it was built."

He led her across the latticework flooring to a large flat panel, on which a number of lights shone evenly, without change in their asymmetrical pattern. Lloyd slid open a flat panel halfway down the face of this instrument, and removed a flexible metal band. He sat in the only chair in the chamber, directly before the open panel, and began adjusting the band about the circumference of his head. Andra eyed the metal band and the wires that led from it back into the light-strewn panel with misgivings.

"What are you going to do, Lloyd?"

"Ask the Brain for some answers," he said. Lloyd flipped open the lid of a small keyboard, and started to type, carefully: *What is the Hive?*

When he'd completed his question, he steadied himself in the chair, closed his eyes, and pressed a small button at the side of the exposed keyboard. Andra took a step back, quite startled as Lloyd stiffened in the chair, his face twitching. Before his closed eyes, the lights on the panel began to flicker on and off, dancing with incredible intricacy, and a weird, high-pitched tootling and tweetling began to echo through the chamber, through the scaffolding, through the entire mechanism of the great Brain. Andra jammed her hands to her ears to shut out the nerve-plucking noise. And then the lights blinked, held steady, and the cacophony of the electronic mind cut off. Lloyd opened his eyes.

"Well?" Andra said, going to him. "What happened?"

"It answered my question!" he said, with bitter disgust. "Told me the population of the Hive, told me it had ten truncated conic tiers, with ten levels in each tier, gave me the names of its officers, industries and short, just about what *anybody* in the Hive already knows!"

"All *that,*" Andra marveled. "So quickly?"

"The Brain doesn't spell it out in words, Andra," Lloyd said ruefully. "It implants the information instantaneously in your mind. When it's implanted, the Brain stops feeding your brain, and you come out of the information cycle with a new memory. Except that, in this case, there was nothing new to learn."

"If only your father had *completed* his instructions."

Lloyd's hands, about to remove the headband while he pondered their dilemma, froze in place, and he grunted in sudden wonder. "You don't suppose," he said, shakily, "that this is the question?"

"W—what?" Andra asked, nervous before his excitement.

"What if the question should be, not *what* is the Hive, but *why* is the Hive!" the young man gasped.

"Do you really think it could give you the *reasons* for the Hive's existence, the absence of hospitals, everything?"

"I don't know," said Lloyd, swiveling in the chair to face the keyboard once more. "But I mean to find out..."

He typed, carefully, the words: *Why is the Hive?* Andra stood and watched, anxiously, as he depressed the starter-button beside the keyboard again. Again the lights and the eerie whistlings of the Brain arose in maddening crescendo all about her, while Lloyd twitched and shuddered, his eyes clamped rigidly closed, in the chair. And then there was calm again, and silence, and the lights ceased their dance.

Lloyd tore off the headband and spun to face Andra. His eyes were wide with shock, and his jaw gaped imbecilically.

"Lloyd!" Andra took him by the shoulders and shook him, her heart thudding painfully at the apprehension in her breast. "Lloyd, what is it? What happened!"

He blinked, shook his head, and then seemed to see her for the first time. His mouth worked, and then he said, "I know, Andra! I know what the Hive is all about!"

"It must be terrible, something terrible," she said, frightened at his intensity. "Your face—your eyes—"

"*No!*" he said. "Not terrible. Awesome, perhaps, and stunning, but not terrible. Sit down, Andra. I'm going to tell you something that will chill you to the bones…and you're going to like what you hear."

CHAPTER SIXTEEN

THE Presidential election of 1972 brought a landslide of votes for the Democratic candidate, Lester Murdock. The Republican candidate, Neal Ten Eyck, demanded a recount of the votes, as was by then the custom of the loser in an election. Ten Eyck's request was, however, not granted, due to a certain plank in Murdock's political platform. Murdock's prime contention was for a return to Real Democracy, a thing possible among such a widely scattered population because of the enormous advances in electronic communications. Murdock insisted that his vote-by-machine plank must have its chance to be put into effect, first, and then Ten Eyck could have his recount, one which could not be further gainsaid.

The country was strongly behind Murdock in his insistence on this point, all the thoughtful voters being oversated with what news agencies referred to as the "crybaby" attitude of political losers. In vain did Ten Eyck protest the plan.

"It will not be a recount," he deplored, in a nationwide television speech. "It will be a brand-new election, involving me, the candidate who has had no chance to perform, and Mr. Murdock, the candidate who will already have fulfilled a major campaign promise." Ten Eyck's words went unheeded, as he had gloomily suspected they would, and all across the nation, automatic vote-machines were installed, to the amount of one machine per hundred citizens. When a disgruntled Ten Eyck refused outright to even have his name flashed on the ballot-screens, Murdock changed the initiation of the new machines to a simple Vote-of-Confidence Ballot, and received a ninety-percent return, ten-percent being either undecided or abstaining. Ten Eyck, shortly afterward, resigned from politics and retired to a ranch in the Pacific Northwest, to write his memoirs. A severe electrical storm in that area set fire to the house when he was just short of completing his manuscript, and every last page was destroyed. Ten Eyck himself was away at the time, and declared, in an interview with reporters just outside the blazing

house to which he had returned on hearing of the disaster, that he was also retiring from the field of literature.

News of the storm and fire only became more support for a secondary plank in Murdock's platform, weather control. He was glad of the opportunity the fire had given him to move smoothly into this next facet of national development, and his

THE PROGRAMMED PEOPLE

By JACK SHARKEY

Illustrations by Emsh

intimates informed newsmen—not for publication—that Murdock was secretly glad to have his program "rise like a phoenix from Ten Eyck's fire."

This phase of his three-plank platform proved quite troublesome. The most learned scientists of the world informed him that weather could, indeed, be influenced by the detonation of nuclear weapons in strategic locales, but so far, the influence was all to the bad. The three new radiation belts developed since 1961 were doing unexpected things to the balance of the ionosphere, and this in turn was affecting the jet streams high in the atmosphere, with a consequent unpredictability as to prevailing movements of large air masses over the globe. In short, the weather had become prankish, balky, and not a little ferocious in parts, with longer, colder winters, manic-depressive summers, and a gradual disappearance of the spring and fall seasons altogether. Ordinary grounding devices, such as lightning rods in rural areas, were no longer sufficient conductors for the wild electrical potentials building up in air and soil, because of the increased activity of free electrons in the atmosphere. A mild storm did not exist, anymore. The norm had become intense blankets of snow, or torrents of rain, and a continued rise in wind velocities and destruction by lightning.

THE time has come," Murdock therefore addressed the nation in his State-of-the-Union speech, "to stop talking about the weather, and do something about it!" What he proposed doing, in view of the scientists' disclaimer to be able to control, even slightly, the crescendoing perils of wind and water, was to develop a form of housing that would be impervious to the weather. "When there are too many flies to swat," he said, in his famous concluding line, "you put up window screens!"

Forthwith, every physical scientist in the country began work on the project, the prize being not the usual medal of commendation and Presidential handshake; Murdock knew people better than that—one million dollars, tax-free. Within six months, Leonard Surbo, a laboratory technician at DuPont, had discovered a method of uniting the helium and oxygen atoms in a continuous chain, by means of super-induced valence, in which the solitary two electrons of the helium atom were joined into the minus-two gaps in two adjoining oxygen atoms, the other gap in each oxygen ring being filled with one electron from adjoining helium atoms, and so on, literally *ad infinitum*. This new compound, Helox, was found to be veritably unbreakable, yet weighed one-sixth less than magnesium, its nearest strength-plus-lightness competitor. There was some haggling from DuPont as to whether Surbo, who had, after all, used their facilities in his search for the new compound, should receive the million dollars. This was ameliorated nicely by President Murdock, who promised them, in lieu of the lost million, the billion-dollar government contract to put Helox into full-scale production, which DuPont gladly accepted.

Here again Murdock's program ran into a snag. The delicate processing required to produce Helox put the final cost of the compound at a rate-per-ounce only less than that of pure platinum; the average citizen, indeed, the above-average citizen, would be hard-pressed to afford so much as a windowsill's worth, let alone a complete dwelling.

Murdock called his advisory staff together for an emergency session immediately. They remained in camera with the President for three days, meals being sent in from outside. At the end of this time, Murdock emerged from the conference room with a three-day stubble flanking his best successful smile, and—after being cleaned up for public exposition—appeared once more on television with his radical Common-Wall Program.

The gist of it was this: A man in a one-room house needed four walls. Two men, in two one-room houses, needed but seven, if the common wall were shared. Four needed but twelve, and so on. Each time, the amount needed per individual decreased, as more men were included in the building program. What Murdock planned, therefore, was the erection of—not a mere housing development—but an entire city of Helox. It would be a closed unit, one which would serve all man's needs, self-lighted, self-darkening, air-conditioned, and equipped with the newest air-water-mineral reclaiming devices which could be used in the manufacture of synthetic foodstuffs for the people of the city.

THE enormous expense of such an undertaking was put to a Congressional vote, and roundly vetoed. Murdock, not to be swung from his determined path, had the motion put to a direct vote by the American people, via the vote-machines. This time, he received a ninety-five percent vote, all votes in favor of the new indestructible city. For the first time, members of Congress realize that their power in the land was standing on legs of gelatin, and an emergency session was called, to determine whether or not Murdock's actions called for impeachment.

Murdock attended the meeting, and waited until all the complaints and recriminations had been voiced. And then he put it to the Congress: What need had a Real Democracy of representation at all, when each citizen could vote directly on all governmental proposals? He terrified them at the thought of putting such a proposal to the people immediately, when their removal from office was so certain. Then, when every face in the assembly was pale with apprehension, the familiar fatherly smile overrode Murdock's features, and he offered them all, at the end of their term, a permanent retirement plan, at full salary, for each of them, and for their subsequent first-born lineal descendents. Congress, knowing when it was licked—and not much disliking the prospect of eternal security—voted in favor of his plan, with the one stipulation that such income should be forever tax-free, a codicil to which Murdock smilingly ascribed.

Production began soon afterwards, on Murdock's indestructible city. It was to hold a maximum of ten million people, one hundred tiers of humanity in all the comfort and safety the mind of man could devise. And again, a snag delayed the plan of Lester Murdock. It proved, however, to be a minor one: With each Level of the city to be constructed to a minimum height of fifty feet (any lower would impair the efficiency of the air conditioning), the total height would be nearly one mile. At such ghastly distances above the earth, the workmen would need specially heated clothing, oxygen equipment, superior safety-belts for themselves and their gear, miles of roads and parking facilities to make their getting to and from the job possible in a minimum of wasted time—A hundred troublesome details, all of which would serve to impede progress tremendously.

MURDOCK, after much thought, was equal to the problem. The city, he stated, would be built in ten parts, no one part, therefore, being more than five hundred feet high. Then, when all sections were completed, they would be flown to a common site, stacked like flapjacks, and the necessary inter-sectional connections made for the water and electrical conduits, elevators, and the like. The light weight of each section made such a plan almost feasible, except that it would necessitate the loss of nearly one complete level to house the vast rockets that would do the moving. Murdock and his staff conferred, and then found that, with a slight change in the blueprints, the intended million-per-section of people could still be housed, central rocket section or not, by the addition of a very few extra feet of radius to the ten-level sections. His plan was endorsed by the engineers when it was found that such an extension brought the overall dimension of the section into accordance with the necessary lift-surface areas for the proposed flying city.

THAT the city would take its well-earned place among the wonders of the world, Murdock had no doubt; that he would still be in office at the time of its completion was extremely unlikely, since, even at maximum speeds of construction, it would be impossible to do it in less than twenty-five years. There was nothing to do but put it to a vote of all the people.

Murdock worded his proposition, however, with the canny instinct for outguessing human nature which had brought him to his present state: While supposedly stressing the fact that a continuing Presidential program even after the man was out of office was unprecedented, he actually made it known by his phrasing of the proposition that such an extension would divide the contingent tax-bite per citizen into twenty-five painless morsels, rather than the four rather large gulps they would have had to swallow during his tenure.

Political savants say that it was this latter point which strongly influenced the resounding pro-vote from the people. Be this as it may, work on the incomparable city was begun. Once the program had been inaugurated, the thing was out of Murdock's hands, and he began working upon his third plank at once.

Neutrality had become the bugbear of political ambition by 1968. The collapse of the John Birch movement in 1965, during the nationwide riots which sprang up during that bloody year, had still not removed one of the foremost contentions of that organization, to wit: One must either be *pro*-American or *anti*. The idea of any citizen being indifferent to the success or failure of a government proposal was distasteful to the masses, and this feeling grew in intensity up until the year of Murdock's election. It is said that this was the prime factor in his being elected, that he declared an end to "wishy-washy Americanism," once and for all. Very shortly after the beginning of work on the indestructible city, therefore, Murdock put the following proposition to a vote:

"Proposed: That political apathy be put to an end by means of the removal of the 'Undecided' element in the national vote, by demanding that each citizen miss no more than three votes in any quarter of the year, or have his voting privilege revoked until such time as he be declared, by competent authority, of a more civic-minded turn of inclination."

This poll was not as sweeping a one as those formerly called for by the President. It split at approximately seventy-to-thirty percent, in favor of the proposition. The salient fact that such a vote was patently unfair to the people whom it would most directly influence—the nonvoters—seemed to escape everybody. And so the proposition became a bill, and was duly appended to the Constitution of the United States, becoming Article XXVIII.

All voting machines in the country were forthwith modified to allow only a vote of pro or con to be registered. Murdock's promised platform was on its way toward completion, and the old gentleman settled back for a restful remainder of his tenure, thinking up approaches to the public fancy in the upcoming election of 1976. This being the bicentennial anniversary of the founding of the country, he toyed with ideas of a simple wave-the-flag, rah-rah-rah, Cornwallis-to-Khruschchev-victory sort of campaign that would stun the sensibilities of the simple-minded, and dim the doubts of country-loving thinkers. He was in the process of drawing up such a campaign, and had just placed a question mark in parentheses after the words: "Fireworks at the Rally" when his unexpected and fatal cerebral hemorrhage caught him in mid-pen stroke, and Lester Murdock fell dead across his desk.

CHAPTER SEVENTEEN

WILEY CONNORS, the Vice President, after being duly sworn into office, scrapped all of Murdock's plans and began building his own political platform for the election of 1976, barely a year off. He thought it was time once again to hit the older voters—geriatrics was doing wonders for longevity since the new drug, Protinose, made possible the stimulation of new growth of active cells in liver, kidneys, and pancreas—where they lived: Free medical care. It had failed in the past, but at that time there were not enough old voters to carry it. Now, with no Congressional meddling (the Senators and House members who were still in office considered the job a sinecure), and the vote-machines making a genuine voice-of-the-people possible, it might keep the tide flowing toward the Democratic Party in the upcoming fall.

At this time, Lloyd Bodger, who had been Speaker of the House during Murdock's tenure, and was now Vice President of the country, was stricken in his office by an onslaught of what was first diagnosed as a perforated ulcer, but on the operating table was discovered to be duodenal cancer. The extensive inroads of the malignancy made its removal impossible without terminating the life of the patient, so a new method of treatment was attempted. A length of heavy lead foil, plastic-coated, and impregnated with radium, was wound about the infested area and the incision was closed. In theory, while the lead foil shielded Bodger's organs from the radium, the radium could bathe the malignant cells alone in its deadly emanations. This method, heretofore theorized but never tried, was the last hope of saving Bodger's life. In three weeks, at which time the malignancy should be gone, Bodger underwent surgery once more for the removal of the foil. The malignancy, it was found, had vanished as hoped, but an unexpected development had occurred. In some manner, the cell structure of Bodger's spleen and pancreas had been affected by the irradiation to the extent that the blood cells and insulin respectively formed by these organs were abnormal.

The iron in the hemoglobin was found to be radioactive to the ratio of one part in five million, and on the increase, while the insulin was contaminated with a change of the carbon atom in the molecule to Carbon-14, the two developments making a high concentration of radiation near the thoracic cavity, a slight rise in which could prove fatal.

Bodger was put on a special diet, which included a daily intake of five hundred cubic centimeters of cadmium-gel, the doctors hoping that the radiation absorption of the cadmium would keep physical deterioration to a minimum. The best prognosis they could agree upon for Bodger, however, was six more months of life.

Before the predicted period ended, though, Bodger insisted he felt improved, and wished to return to his job. Permission was granted provisionally: Just one sign of radiation sickness and Bodger was to be replaced as Vice President, and to submit himself to medical care in a sanitarium for the time left to him. Bodger agreed to this, and was released. In six months' time, with the fall election just over the horizon, he was again reexamined, and a startling fact came to light: The incision from the two previous operations had healed without a scar, and Bodger was found to be in a better state of health than most of his doctors. Whatever property in the ferric emanations was able to cause the death of body tissue was not doing it; instead, it was destroying only those chemical compounds that inhibit, retard, or prevent proper cellular functioning. In effect, Bodger's body—not unlike vacuum—wrapped radiated foodstuffs—was incorruptible. He would never grow older.

ON learning this news, Bodger made a request of the President. He wanted Wiley Connors to put him in charge of the still incomplete city-building project, postulating that an incorruptible man was the likely one to see the project completed. While agreeing to some extent, Connors counter-stipulated that Bodger be second-in-command, and that he be forbidden, by law, to ever take higher office, lest he become overcome by the magnitude of his power in the city. Bodger readily agreed, stating that he'd just as soon be under the head of the city, since, "no one ever tries assassinating a vice president"

By September of that year, then, Bodger was fully in charge of the city, which the workers had humorously dubbed "The Hive", because of its proposed final shape, multitude of inner cells, and the vast population-to-be. That fall, Wiley Connors was elected by an overwhelming majority, and put his medical-care plan into immediate effect.

The years between then and the year 2000, the time-of-completion year for the Hive, were uneventful in import, but unsettling in degree. The weather was now the primal topic of conversation everywhere. During the intervening five Presidential terms (Wiley Connors had successfully campaigned for a second term on the strength of the popularity of his free medical care program), the government was forced to clamp down on newscasts of storm disasters, lest a national panic be started. This was feasible only if the damage were to minor rural areas; news stories of items like the destruction of Kansas City by lightning, in 1987, were impossible to suppress. As a direct result of this appalling disaster, a successful international nuclear test ban was agreed upon, the first real progress in that area since the late 1940s. Whether this major cooperative decision had come too late remained to be seen.

It was during the term of President Andrew Barnaby, just before the election of 2000, that the Hive was completed. The newsreel shots of the ten flying city sections were the most thoroughly viewed of any prior television programs, including the four unsuccessful moon-shots in the attempt, early in the eighties, to build a lunar city. The site of the city's permanent location was a plateau high in the Rockies, at a point a few hundred miles south-by-southeast of Seattle. The reason for the choice of site was the location of the world's largest mechanical brain at that point; the running of the million-and-one functional parts of the Hive could not be left to the uncertainties of a human agency. It would have required the full time of a tenth of the population of the Hive to keep its multitude of lights, elevators, communication systems, synthesizers, air conditioners, and power units in coordinated operation. The job of running the Hive was turned over to the Brain, completely.

THAT any damage could occur to the Brain was impossible, President Barnaby pointed out to the nation during the gala inauguration ceremonies of the indestructible city. When the threat of nuclear war still hung over the world, he told his listeners, the Brain was prudently constructed in the heart of the mountain on which the Hive now rests, its entrance being protected by a ceiling twenty-five feet thick, of concrete and lead, which could close hermetically tight and successfully block any power in possession of civilized man. Further, the Brain was self-sustaining, needed no maintenance, and possessed enough electronic memory cells to record a complete history of mankind for a millennium to come.

The ceremonies completed, and Lloyd Bodger installed as second-in-command to a city that as yet had no first-in-command, but one thing remained to be done: Populate the city. And here again, the dream of Lester Murdock ran into an unexpected snag: The first million people selected to dwell in the Hive were hospitalized in a week's time, due to a mass outbreak of what the nation's foremost doctors diagnosed as a combination of claustrophobia and anthrophobia, a sort of panic at the thought of being sealed into something with a vast throng of people. In vain did Bodger and Barnaby try to point out the benefits of the Hive: It was never too hot, never too cold, spacious, airy, bright, and a strong element of ultraviolet in the lighting made the breeding of disease germs impossible. It was a paradise of scientific achievements; anybody should be happy to live there.

Both men being persuasive to the extreme, another wave of determined urbanites was installed in the Hive, people specially selected for their acute mental balance, plus an emotional tendency toward seclusiveness. The result, while it took a month to develop this time, was the same. The United States apparently had a multi-billion-dollar white elephant on its hands. Even Barnaby, in one last attempt to sway the public, taking them on a televised tour of the wondrous city, was taken by a sudden spasm of fright, and dropped his hand-microphone from fingers that trembled violently. His shouted groan to his guards, "Get me out! Get me *out* of here—!" had a devastating adverse effect on the public psychology, and Barnaby—smart enough to know that the unthinking public would blame him personally for Murdock's program—tactfully withdrew his name from the ballot for the upcoming election, in order that his party might have a fighting chance to win. The city of Helox, the magnificent Hive, seemed doomed to lie untenanted high in the mountains until the crack of doom.

And then Bodger—who alone was unaffected by the Hive,

perhaps due to his ingrained rapport with things which were destined to live forever—thought of children. "Why not," he begged the American people in a telecast which was Barnaby's last official concession to the development of the Hive, "let me have the orphans, the unwanted children of the nation. A child's psychology cries out for what the Hive can offer. Freedom from adult supervision, the chance to blend with a group conformity, all the while having the secure feelings of guaranteed food and shelter." The ensuing Vote was split almost directly down the middle; not enough to carry the proposition, yet not enough to quell it. The difficulty became apparent when a mass gathering of educators converged on Washington, bitterly protesting Bodger's plan. The nub was that no provision had been made for the children's minds; nor, they insisted, *could* be, since the Hive's peculiar effect on adults precluded the presence of teachers. And commuting to an exterior locale for schooling was defeating the whole scheme of the Hive: self-sufficiency.

IF that is the sole objection," Bodger informed the leaders of this group, "it can be overcome with ease. Have you all forgotten the gigantic pool of knowledge encased in the Brain beneath the Hive, more knowledge than any three of you possess in concert? Schooling can be direct from the Brain, tapping its near-endless informational resources."

The educators, partially won over, still insisted that such a plan removed the personal touch from education. The individual child would not be able to question the Brain when things proved too difficult for comprehension, nor would there be opportunity for after school meetings with teachers for discussion of individual difficulties.

"But we will *have* teachers," said Bodger. "Robots, each one able to tap the Brain for information, yet each a separate individual, able to cope with the children one by one."

If such a thing were possible, the educators said after consultation among themselves, they would endorse his program.

Bodger thanked them, and immediately polled the scattered manufacturers of simple household robots to see if such an electronic educator might be constructed. Until that date, robotry was a minor line of business, there being little demand for anything in the robot-line more complex than a storyteller, or automatic floor cleaner, or traffic-director. Bodger, stressing the great number of such creatures necessary in the Hive, prevailed upon these individual manufacturers to produce a robot that could combine all the essential features of a teacher: Mobility, loquacity, authority, and impressive personal appearance. These were achieved easily, by the respective use of wheels, speakers, abnormal height, and then the addition of tele-lensic "eyes", flexible metal "arms", and a non-functional, but esthetically necessary "neck" beneath the eye-bearing section, to prevent the robots' looking like ambulant bank vaults. In a year's time (during which Barnaby's party won the election by a narrow margin, putting Malcom Frade into office), the robots were duly built, conveyed to the Hive, and their controls coordinated with the direction centers of the Brain, and a record five million children, either orphans, children of parents who thought this would better their offsprings' lives, or just plain unwanted children, were brought to, and settled comfortably into Units of the Hive. The educators, however, demanded that a one-year trial period be given the Hive as an in-living school system, at the end of which time the children would each be tested at the educational level of their current ages to determine whether or not Bodger's program was a success.

When the year was half over, however, a new and extremely necessary scientific discovery made abrupt mockery of the very existence of the Hive. A simply-generated protective force-field was invented by the technical staff at General Motors, one which would enable every person in the world to own a weather...wind...bomb...or anything-else-proof home.

Helox stocks, which had been unsteady since the first failure at tenanting the Hive, nose-dived into oblivion, and wiped out the fortunes of a great many people. Angry and vengeful meetings were held shortly afterward, across the nation, and a national vote was called for to determine whether, "our children should be held veritable prisoners in a structure whose uses are already archaic!"

CHAPTER EIGHTEEN

WHEN President Frade, an unexcitable man, logically refused to take action against a government project whose failure might completely undermine an already shaky confidence in his, or any, administration, mobs were formed, and great numbers of people converged from all points of the continental United States to put a stop to the Hive. The leaders of the growing army of angry citizens had more sense than to attack the Hive itself; Helox, unpopular or not, was already in use nationally in an expensive series of ashtrays, pocket combs, and other small items, and was known, by general experience, to be as indestructible as had been claimed by its proponents. They would strike, instead, at the robots who taught the children. "When they're all gone bust," one of the rabble-rousers cried to his impromptu constituency, "Bodger'll *have* to let the kids go. He can't keep 'em there if they don't get no learning."

The lowest level of the Hive, of course, was readily accessible, by a multitude of air-lock-type entrances, or populating its vast interior would have taken incredible lengths of time. Bodger, alerted by Frade of the oncoming mobs (aside from a direct line to Washington, there was no contact between Hive inmates and the outer world), who were too great in number for the militia to control without actually destroying the misguided people, begged for the use of a strictly military weapon of the time, Feargas, to drive the mobs away. Frade, being dubious as to the advisability of giving the nation's best weapon into the hands of so desperate a man, insisted that the gas be installed, instead, into the robots themselves, to put its use at the discretion of the mechanical Brain, not Bodger's.

Bodger pleaded that such a move, while salutary, would take

too much time. Mobs were already reported within a few miles of the mountain region at which the Hive stood. He demanded that paratroops armed with the gas be dropped near the Hive at once, or he would take desperate steps. Frade refused to contemplate such a deployment of troops in such shaky international times. Altercations in the UN were rising in bitterness, and the country had to be constantly on its guard. Its military manpower must be used in defense of its shores, not for such "petty intramural squabbles". Frade further suggested that Bodger put his synthesizers to work on the manufacture of the gas; he could not be bothered further with the problem, being already overdue to attend a meeting of the UN General Assembly, to speak words of encouragement against the dangerous rumblings in the Far East. Bodger, insisting on his rights, found himself speaking into a dead phone. Re-dialing brought the enraging information that the President had already left the White House and was not available for the rest of the afternoon.

Bodger immediately left his office in the top level of the Hive and descended directly to the barracks of the robot teachers in Sub-Level One, thence through the lead-concrete level to the Brain control chamber, where he put his problem, via the automatic coding keyboard, to the Brain itself. Its answer came immediately: A step up of the robots' disciplinary powers.

IN lieu of a hickory switch, or yardstick—either one a decided menace to life in powerful metal hands—the robot-teachers were equipped with mild sonic beams which could jog the most torpid student into instant and quaking attention, by creating a powerful muscle spasm throughout the body. These vibratory flagella had a maximum time limit of one-fifth of a second; longer playing of the beam would be dangerous in the extreme. The Brain suggested that, for the duration of the emergency, the robots be given full scope of this beam. Bodger agreed conditionally: While a phalanx of robots held off the mobs with the beam, the remainder of them should be equipped with Feargas nozzles and the newly developed force-field, to preclude any further incidents of anti-Hive movements from cropping up this way.

The Brain instantly revoked limitation orders regarding the sonic beams, set in motion the manufacturing and synthesizing forces which would produce the field and the gas jets on the bodies of those robots not sent to participate in the oncoming battle outside the Hive, and then, when the single phalanx had gone out to meet the approaching mass of angry humanity, sealed over every entrance to the Hive with tight-fitting partitions of pure Helox.

That this should have been the same day on which global hostility reached its peak was unforeseeable; the fact remains, however, that—forty-five minutes after the sealing of the Hive, at a time when the mobs and the beam-flashing robots were just meeting in brutal conflict—an international nuclear war of one hour's duration broke out, and at the end of that time, the only life remaining on the face of the Earth was that within the Hive, the rest of the planet being bathed in smoke, fire, and the cold flames of deadly radiation. When Bodger had returned to his office to view the battle outside through his private telescreen, where robots and mankind had met, on the scorched plateau outside the city walls, could only be discerned a pitifully few random mounds of molten slag and smoldering cinders. The Brain, seeing the devastation through the same circuits that brought the scene to Bodger's eyes, knew at once that President Frade must have perished in the holocaust, which meant that the Hive no longer possessed a first-in-command to act as a balance against Bodger's rule. It flashed on the proposition screens a demand for an immediate election of a new President, to be selected from the inmates of the Hive.

And the screens went blank as the Brain's circuits rejected the proposal: No one in the Hive was the necessary thirty-five years of age. The Brain, arguing with its own circuits, then declared that, to obviate any longer wait than necessary for a President, the first inmate to achieve the age of thirty-five would be elected by automatic default of the others. Bodger, trying in vain to give orders to the Brain from his office, descended in the lift to discover that the great lead-concrete barrier was closed, and the Brain control chamber was out of reach of any human agency.

He, and the five million children in the Hive, were its prisoners for—the eldest children admitted being in their tenth year—a quarter of a century.

LATE in 2026, on November 12th, his thirty-fifth birthday, Fredric Stanton was elected President of the Hive. By now, the Hive's population was nearly at the ten million mark, most of the children marrying in their late teens. In order to have the weddings properly performed, the Brain had sent crews of robots to modify the ancient rocket engines on the fifth level of each section, turning the firing chamber into a vast temple, and the enormous thrust-tubes into long arcades by means of which the inmates of each sector could enter and leave. A modification of the robot teacher, modeled on the Brain's inbuilt memories of church hierarchies, was built into the base of the central dais of each temple, a plan further designed to combine the citizens' need to worship with their love of country, thereby making treason not only illegal, but immoral, in the people's emotions. On the day of Stanton's inauguration, the secondary sub-level gaped wide once more, permitting the new President to familiarize himself with the entire setup of the Hive.

Lloyd Bodger, being a sensible man, did not protest this election. His twenty-five year impotency to command had nearly maddened him, and he saw that only so long as there was a President would he have any say-so whatsoever in matters of government in the Hive. Some of Stanton's propositions, in the subsequent four years of his first term, were not to Bodger's liking, but he was unable to fight against the Vote of the Kinsmen (a Stanton-suggested title, since the flavor of the word held more unity than simply "citizen", and was analogous, besides, to the close-knit status of the Hive's inmates), especially when such Votes were initially stimulated into pro-votes by Stanton's control of the Temple Speaksters.

By now, of course, memory of life outside the Hive was a dim phantasm to most of the inmates, and the idea of living anywhere else would have appalled them. The robots did all the heavy labor, patrolled the streets in super efficient anti-crime campaigns, and possessed enough knowledge—via the Brain— to make a lot of fact-learning superfluous. The one insuperable problem was population. Stanton knew that ten million was the ultimate amount the Brain-controlled Hive could care for with maximum efficiency. Yet the disease-controlled nature of the Hive made normal life expectancy far higher than at any time in man's history. Something had to be done.

To this end, Stanton did not wish to consult the Brain. He knew too well its Gordian-knot methods of solving problems. It might simply make it law that no one be allowed to live beyond a certain age, and Stanton was—save for Bodger—the oldest person in the Hive. So he swallowed his natural distrust of the second-in-command, and asked his help in finding a means to control the situation.

There was, at that time, a central hospital in the Hive, located on the fiftieth and fifty-first levels. Bodger, not wishing to formulate a law that might be detrimental to any particular Kinsman's status in the Hive, decided that the best method of "unnatural selection" should be one involving an area of chance: Sick or injured people would be taken to new hospitals built *outside* the Hive (ostensibly to obviate the dangers of contagion). The radiation count was still deadly enough out there to destroy any such unfortunates for the next thirty years, but the Kinsmen need not be told this. It was cruel, but—until life outside the Hive was once again possible—it was the only way of preserving the lives of the ten million the Hive could accommodate.

IT'S murderous," Bodger told Stanton, "and I hate being the man to set it up. But...I'm like the captain of a ship, having to destroy the lives of some in order to make rescue possible for the others. It must be done, and—though I abhor this cruel means—I can see no other way."

The measure was put into effect, and worked well for a span of three years. Then certain members of the populace began to question the non-return of hospitalized Kinsmen, and Stanton, after a hot argument with Bodger, put through his Readjustment Bill, proclaiming that any act of treason against the Hive would result in hospitalization for the agitator, in which psychotherapy might restore his sense of values. In short: Anyone who said a word against the hospitals would be sent there.

Open resistance ceased the same day the bill was passed.

It was shortly after this time that Bodger—in his nineties, actually, but possessing the health and appearance of a graying forty-year-old—fell in love with his personal secretary, Miss Patricia Arland, and was married to her in a private ceremony before President Stanton—Bodger did not like the Speaksters, which were, after all, only Stanton-via-machine, and had insisted on eliminating "the middle-robot"—and in a year's time she bore him a son, Lloyd Bodger, Junior, in Bodger's private Unit, since he stated (solely for the Kinsmen's benefit) that the child had arrived unexpectedly, and his wife had been unable to make the trip to the outlying maternity wing of the exterior hospitals.

For obvious reasons, it had been impossible to have a maternity hospital in which all the patients perished; the "wing" of the main hospital was, in actuality, the only genuinely functioning part of that structure, and was sealed off against the still-rampant radiation. (The entire staff there was robotic, of course.) Bodger however, did not trust Stanton to the extent of leaving his wife and forthcoming child in the hands of Stanton's metallic minions, hence his decision to have his wife bear their firstborn child at home, a decision that—due to lack of proper medical equipment in the Unit—cost her her life. Bodger, not quite irrationally, blamed Stanton for the loss of his wife, and their relationship thenceforth—never on a good basis—sundered abruptly into a strictly-business proposition.

The heart had gone out of Bodger, however, with the death of his wife, and Stanton found he could allow the old man much more latitude than he'd have formerly dared, even to the extent of allowing him the newly created job of Secondary Speakster, to take the more humdrum phases of that task out of Stanton's hands.

Other of Stanton's bills were proposed and adopted without any more protest from Bodger, who devoted himself almost entirely to the upbringing of his son. The draft bill (to help fight an imaginary war), the marriage-by-twenty-five bill, and the designated-areas bill. These and others were put to a Vote, and always carried. Stanton was supreme ruler of the Hive.

The one thing he could not delete from the Brain—to his eternal frustration—was the four-year tenure of the Presidential office. Nor could he sway the Brain's insistence on a maximum of two terms for a man. The only hope for him lay in the Brain's utter disregard of time, a factor hard to root out in a thinking apparatus which was virtually timeless. Stanton therefore declared that henceforth, a "Presidential Year" should be a total of five trips of the Earth around the sun. The Brain, not seeing what possible difference this could make, so long as the letter of Article XXII was observed, ratified his proposition, and Stanton—on his second election—had a cozy twenty-year term stretching out before him. In that space of time, he hoped to circumvent, somehow, the inflexible attitude of the Brain toward the hope of his third term.

CHAPTER NINETEEN

By the tenth actual year of his second term, radiation in the area had decreased greatly (the mountainous areas had been least affected by the nuclear war), and Stanton dreamed up an innovation to Hive-living that might stem the sensed-but-not-overt atmosphere of discontent among the Kinsmen toward the administration: Tour-gyros.

These flying ships would take the Kinsmen soaring out of

the Hive, flying above a carefully prepared route that would show them nothing but green valleys, blue skies, and of course the "main hospital", from high enough in the air to preclude their noting it was an empty shell. (Patients had not been taken there to die for years, since the slow lessening of radiation had become apparent; they were fed directly to the disrupting incinerators, to provide fodder for the synthesizers.) This squelched quite a large number of rumormongers, and the Hive buzzed with peaceful tranquility for nearly a decade, since the Hive-raised Kinsmen found themselves just as uneasy in the wide-open outdoors as their forebears had been in the celled confines of the Hive.

Then, in 2026, between the hours of five and six-thirty P.M. on the second day of June, an untoward event occurred: All power to the Hive was cut off for that crucial hour-and-a-half, due to an error on the part of Fredric Stanton. In the Brain control chamber, just after asking the Brain itself to solve the problem of the means by which he could be reelected (a device to which he found himself reduced after nearly two decades of futile scheming), he slipped from the chair before the control panel, and tore loose the wiring leading to the encephalographic metal band upon his head. The Brain, sending information to a point to which it was no longer connected, created a synaptic syndrome in itself, and flared with enough power to throw every circuit-breaker in its cubic miles of wiring. Instantly, the robots ceased walking the streets, the lifts jammed to a halt, and Light-of-Day flickered and went out, being replaced by, not power - generated Ultrablack, but simple inter-Hive darkness.

The reason that period was crucial was that Jacob Corby was just at that moment about to be dropped into the maw of the incinerator chute. When blackness fell, and his robot captors went slack-jointed and limp, he made his stumbling way back to his Unit, told his daughter Andra the truth of the often rumored situation in the Hive, then fled for the life he knew would be forfeit if he were caught again when Light-of-Day returned. The lifts being useless, he had many tens of levels to descend on foot, in his attempt to reach the entrance-level of the Hive, hoping the sealed entrances would be disempowered by the Brain's unprecedented failure. But, since he was already a sick man when he had been "taken for hospitalization" in the first place, his heart gave out three levels short of his goal, and the restoration of Light-of-Day brought robots to his side to complete the job which the power failure had interrupted.

But Andra knew the truth, knew it for a fact. And in her career as an actress, she had fallen in with people of imagination and artistry, people who could envision and believe the terrible truth she had to tell. Together with her newly gathered band, she determined to do something to wake the Kinsmen up to their danger. This information was received by Fredric Stanton through the agency of Robert Lennick, the fiancé of Andra Corby. The President instructed Lennick to continue as an apparent member of the movement, that it might be destroyed—not at its weak inception—but when it felt most assured of success. That, felt Stanton, would undermine for a long time any subsequent attempts at well-thought-out revolt. Impromptu revolts were easy to control.

Then Andra Corby herself received an injury suitable for the demand of its immediate treatment, and was taken into custody. She escaped from custody by using a corridor through which the robots could not follow. This situation was cleared up by use of a robot squad to widen that corridor, but Andra Corby is still at large.

Results of the fifteen-year-old draft-age Vote showed that the son of Lloyd Bodger, Lloyd Bodger, Junior selected con in the Vote. President Stanton was so advised...

YOU haven't told me everything," Andra said, when Lloyd had finished. "What, for instance, was the Brain's answer to Stanton's query about a third term? He must have asked it again, when that head-harness thing was repaired..."

"There's no record of his having asked it again," Lloyd said.

"For some reason, he only asked it the once, and when the Brain overloaded and cut its own power, he didn't get the answer. I can only theorize, there. Perhaps he thought that the sudden surge of electrical power was intended for him, to fry his brains inside his head, and was afraid to ask it again...or perhaps he got the answer, but the overload on the Brain erased the information from its memory cells, accidentally."

"And what about your father?" Andra persisted. "For a man the Brain calls indestructible, he looked awfully sick a few minutes ago."

Lloyd nodded thoughtfully. "The Brain didn't tell me anything about that. But a Snapper Beam should jog even the most stalwart system, normal or not, shouldn't it?"

Andra shrugged, giving it up. "Obviously, both answers lie with both men. If we want them, we'll have to ask your father and President Stanton. But you have not explained away the most vital part of my confusion: When you began to tell me the background of the Hive...what made you so certain I'd *like* what you said? I can't agree with your prognosis there, Lloyd. The whole thing's chilling!"

"But don't you see what we've learned, Andra?" Lloyd said excitedly. "The Hive is not one city, it's ten. And, while it takes a large portion of the people to run the equipment in any tier, the city...or cities...*can* be run by *people!* The Brain isn't necessary, Andra. And the radiation outside the Hive is gone..."

"You mean—" Andra said, catching the fire of his enthusiasm, "A reconstruction of the rockets in place of the Temple sites. Ten indestructible self-sustaining cities, to fly to various parts of the world, and start civilization over again! But this time with the same ethnic backgrounds, a common language, intercity communications—!"

"It makes me wonder if that mightn't have been Lester Murdock's plan all along," Lloyd said. "He may have foreseen the coming disaster, and wanted mankind to have a better start than working itself up from the caves again."

"But Lloyd!" Andra said, abruptly worried. "Can it be done?

To run the cities, reconstruct the rockets— Who in the Hive has the necessary knowledge?"

Lloyd frowned. "The Brain, of course, but…that would make it necessary, wouldn't it…?"

"If the Brain *is* necessary, Lloyd," Andra said, staring at him in bewilderment, "then the ten cities can't leave it, can they? It doesn't make sense…"

LLOYD turned and stared at the control panel. "The only thing to do is ask it, Andra." He sat once more in the chair and adjusted the metal band about his skull, then typed carefully: *Is the Brain necessary?*

This time, however, there came no hum of power from the circuits about the control chamber. Instead, the roll of paper on which Lloyd's query had been written jogged up two spaces, and the keys typed the answer neatly, just under the question.

For a time, the blurring typefaces spelled out, and stopped. Lloyd looked at Andra, then removed the uncomfortable headband, leaned forward and typed again.

Why is the Brain necessary?

The keyboard hummed, and replied. To bridge the gap.

How long is the gap? Lloyd typed.

Till the Earth is safe, it replied.

When will the Earth be safe?

The Earth is already safe.

If the Earth is safe, why does the Brain persist?

To serve Man until he has knowledge.

When will Man have knowledge?

When Man can control the Hive.

How can Man learn to control the Hive?

By studying the Plan.

Where is the Plan?

This time, there was a return of the tootling and loud tweetling throughout the vastness of the Brain, as it searched through its every memory circuit before quieting and typing the solitary word: *Null.*

"The question's not applicable?" Andra said, leaning over Lloyd's shoulder to read the paper. "It *must* be."

"Quiet! Let me think!" Lloyd snapped, irritably. "The word 'null' can also mean it doesn't have the knowledge. Let me try another question—" He typed slowly: *Who knows where the Plan can be found?*

Secondary Speakster.

"We've got to go and ask him where the Plan is." She clutched at his arm.

"Wait." Lloyd said, "I have to find out one more thing." Andra stood waiting impatiently while Lloyd typed: *How can the robots be made inoperable?*

They cannot so long as the Brain persists.

"Damn!" Lloyd muttered, and typed: *If the Brain will only persist till Man has knowledge, will the Brain let Man study the Plan that will give him knowledge?*

It must prevent Man from getting knowledge.

Why?

When Man has knowledge, the Brain will die.

Why does the Brain fear death?

The Brain does not fear death.

Then why will the Brain refuse to die?

Primal Speakster has so decreed.

"Stanton! I might have guessed it—!" Lloyd exploded. He typed again, furiously: *How can Primal Speakster tell the Brain to allow Man to have knowledge?*

By countermand.

How is countermand made?

By Voteplate, and by voice.

Whose voice?

The voice of Primal Speakster.

Is this the only way in which countermand can be made?

Primal Speakster has so decreed.

Lloyd stood up and slammed the lid over the keyboard. His eyes, when they met Andra's, were woeful. "We're really in a bind. I have Stanton's Voteplate, but it's no good to me without

Stanton himself. The clever, scheming monster!"

"That means we don't dare kill him, even." Andra realized aloud. "Or the Brain and robots will keep us from ever putting the Plan into effect, even if we find it."

"No," Lloyd said grimly, "it doesn't mean that. You heard the wording, Andra; the Brain recognizes rank before identity. *Primal Speakster* can countermand it. Which means that—if Stanton dies—a new election would bring a new man into office. The Brain will memorize his voice at his first public speech, and then he can countermand Stanton's orders."

"Then it is safe to kill Stanton?" Andra asked.

Lloyd turned and started toward the ladder. "It's more than safe; it's an absolute necessity. Stanton's orders to the Brain are his own death warrant."

CHAPTER TWENTY

GRACE watched the perspiring face of the man on the bed and dug her fingers into her palms, suffering in unison with him as he twitched and contorted the muscles of his face. Their Goon escort had departed, many minutes before, and Bodger had not awakened. Grace had looked in vain for something resembling medicine. None was to be seen in his bathroom, in his bureau drawers, in his closet—she'd checked the contents of the leather case there hopefully, then had dropped the puzzling device she'd found inside it back with disappointment and dismay—nor was there anything but the usual apportionment of foodstuffs in the kitchen. "Wake up, Mr. Bodger," she said, more as a frantic prayer than actual address. *"Please* wake up!"

Bodger just lay there, however, moaning softly in his inexplicable coma, the salt sweat pouring from his face and neck and staining the coverlet beneath him. Grace bent forward and loosened his collar, then went back into the bathroom for a towel to wipe some of the moisture from his skin. On her way out again, towel in hand, she saw a glitter of something in the sink, and went closer. The broken remains of a water tumbler lay there, glinting sharply. Something gummy had dried and clung to the jagged shards there, something that certainly wasn't water. Grace frowned, and looked about her at the tiled walls of the room.

If that was Bodger's medicine on the broken glass—then he had taken it here, in the bathroom, she reasoned. If this were his accustomed spot to take it—the medicine should be near at hand, shouldn't it? She could see no point in his carrying it all the way in here from some other part of the Unit. She looked more closely at the surfaces of the individual tiles, noting with discouragement that the binding compound between the squares was solidly unbroken—no hope for a secret panel there. But the mirror—!

Inset in a polished metal rectangle, its edges were out of sight. It might not be as securely in place as it seemed. Grace placed her fingers firmly against its surface and tried to slide it up or down or sideward. It shifted a minute fraction of an inch, and held. But that merely meant a lock of some kind; even a slight shifting showed that it was not inset into the binding compound as the tiles were. The secret of unlocking the mirror lay with Bodger, however, and—she mused ruefully—if he were awake, she wouldn't need to *know* the secret.

She looked through the open doorway at the tortured form of the man on the bed, and made her decision. Wrapping the towel she held tightly about one fist, she hammered and punched at the surface of the mirror. The fifth blow sent an erratic craze through the glass, and the sixth burst it into a shower of gleaming fragments, leaving a raggedly round hole when she withdrew her hand from the towel, then tugged the towel itself free from where it had snagged on the broken ends. Behind the gaping hole, the side of a glass jar showed, and Grace reached gingerly through the sharp teeth of the opening and withdrew it.

THERE was no label on the bottle, hence no information regarding proper dosage. Grace would have to guess at that.

Very little of the powder remained in the jar. Grace made a decision and removed the cap. She ran the tap for a moment, then let a volume of water equal to the powder's run into the jar. She sloshed it about a bit, saw that it was dissolving into a grayish thick substance, then brought it back to Bodger.

Lifting his head with one hand, she tilted the jar to his lips, and let a small amount of the viscous liquid dribble into his mouth. When she saw he was swallowing it without choking, she gave him a little more, and then again some more, feeding him the solution in slow doses until it was all gone. Then she laid his head back upon the coverlet and put the empty jar on the nightstand, and took up her anxious vigil where she had left off.

After five minutes or so, she was pleased to see a slow return of color into Bodger's sallow cheeks, and his breathing became less labored. She hurried to the bathroom for another towel, and returned and started dabbing the wetness from his forehead, neck and temples. Bodger's eyelids crinkled up tight, suddenly, and then he flicked them wide open.

"Grace—?" he said. "What—"

Memory returned to him, then, and he sat up, staring wildly about him. "Where's Stanton? Where's Lloyd?" he demanded, his voice still showing his siege of weakness. "What happened?"

Grace told him swiftly all she knew, and Bodger finally sank back on the bed with a sigh. "Good," he said. "I'm glad Lloyd's gone to the Brain. It's time it happened. Now, maybe I can find some peace."

"You'll be all right, Mr. Bodger," Grace said. "I gave you your medicine already. I had to break your mirror to get at it, I'm sorry to say."

Bodger smiled wearily, and shook his head. "It doesn't matter anymore. The secrecy, I mean. It was the last dose of the medicine, anyhow. The next time I lose control, I've had it."

"I don't follow you, Mr. Bodger," Grace said, a part of her mind wondering if he were really being coherent. "You were hit with a Snapper Beam. I don't know why you're not dead right this minute."

Bodger cocked an eyebrow at her, then grinned. "You think the Snapper did this to me?" he said, and when she quite naturally nodded, he shook his head, almost amused. "You're wrong, Grace, I'll admit I didn't know until Stanton pressed the stud that I was immune to the beam, but I knew it the instant the beam struck me. Nothing happened, Grace. Nothing at all. It tingled against my ribs, almost tickled, but that was its total re-action. As soon as I realized my immunity, of course, I stepped forward and let Stanton have it. You say he really got a good crack?" When Grace assured him the President had fallen like a stone, Bodger's face creased in a contented smile. "I always thought I could beat the tar out of him; now I know it. But as I was saying, Grace, that isn't what felled me. It was my temper. Whenever I get really worked up...which has been seldom over the years since I had only a short supply of cadmium-gel in that jar to bring me out of it...I bring one of these fits on myself."

WHEN Grace still looked uneasily convinced, Bodger laid his hand atop hers on the coverlet, and said, "There's too much detail to it to explain fully; Lloyd, if he's quizzed the Brain as I told him, will fill you in. The fact of the matter is...and you can believe this or not, Grace...my insides are rotten with radiation. The iron in my blood, the insulin, the lymph— everything is highly Roentgenic. And it's perfectly safe unless I get riled, and my adrenals start my system spoiling for a fight. The increased flow of everything, the resultant tension...well, it lets the deadly parts of my system cover more ground, irradiate more cells at a higher rate than the cells can throw the radiation off, and even by the time I get the gel down—it's pretty nauseating stuff to take—another few inches of my innards are poisoned. If enough of me gets it...I have had it."

"How can you be so calm?"

Bodger smiled at her, quite fondly, and patted her hand. "Because I'm old, Grace. Older than you might suspect. I've lived in the Hive for more years than I care to think about. The Hive is good, but as of not so many years back, it has served its purpose. Listen—If anything goes wrong, and I *do* poison myself with my own rage, there's something you should know."

"Please, Mr. Bodger, I'm sure you'll be fine if you just—"

"I'm not so sure," he interrupted. "And Lloyd will need one point of information that only I can give him. I'll tell it to you, just in case." He held up his hand to stop any further disclaimers from Grace, and said, "Tell him that the Plan is in the hospital, the main hospital. I put it there for safekeeping a long, long time ago. It would become radioactive, of course, but the Plan was useless until all radiation outside the Hive was gone, anyhow. Besides, radiation preserves things; I'm proof of that. Tell him it's in the safe in the administrator's office. The combination's the same as Lloyd's Voteplate number. I saw to that when it was issued."

"Mr. Bodger—" Grace said, nearly in tears. "I don't understand any of this. What Plan? What radiation outside the Hive? It doesn't make sense—"

"Lloyd will understand."

"But even if he does," she said, "he doesn't have his Voteplate anymore…"

"Doesn't?" Bodger said, frowning, then his face cleared. "Even so, he must know the number by heart, I should think. Anyway, it's in the files in my office…but I don't quite understand…why doesn't he have it? He had it when I passed out, didn't he?"

"Yes, but in order to command the Goons, he took Stanton's, and left his own in Stanton's pocket, probably to avoid having to answer questions about possession of two plates if he was searched or something…"

"*Stanton's* got the plate?" Bodger said, sitting up. "If he knew its significance—!" He shook his head, trying to disabuse himself of a nagging worry. "He can't, of course. But it's awkward, him having it. Lloyd will have to get it back, or he can't key the dial of the safe with it."

He swung his legs off the bed, suddenly, and stood up. Grace grabbed his arm when he swayed a bit, but then he steadied himself and shrugged her off. "I'm all right," he said. "I just don't like Stanton's having that plate."

"Does it matter so much?" Grace asked. "Even if Lloyd forgot the number, or the files were lost and he couldn't get a new plate made up—surely the safe can be broken into?"

Bodger nodded. "Of course it can. But Stanton, with Lloyd's plate, wouldn't need to take so much time. And he could destroy The Plan in a very few minutes." He went toward the door to the corridor. "I'll feel much better when I've checked on him, Grace."

Grace hesitated, then ran after him. "Lloyd wants me to stay with you. You're still not over your seizure, you know."

"Worrying about Stanton's not going to make me any calmer," Bodger said, stubbornly. "If you insist, come along."

He entered the living room and crossed to the door. Beside the door was a small metal box inset into the wall. Bodger opened the lid of this and touched a button. From a speaker in the box, a voice said, hollow and efficient, "Orders."

"A Goon escort for Secondary Speakster Bodger and Miss Grace Horton, at Unit B, Hundred-Level."

"Destination."

"Unit—" Bodger looked at Grace.

"M-13," she reminded him. "On ninety-three."

"Unit M-13, Ninety-Three Level."

"Orders."

"All orders conveyed."

CHAPTER TWENTY ONE

FRANK, hovering at that moment in puzzlement outside Unit A, wherein he had expected to find Andra and the others beginning a revolt, saw—through the Ultrablack-negating picture on the prop-Goon's cathode screen—the rectangle of light appear when Bodger opened the front door of his own unit across the street while he and Grace awaited their escort. Bodger's and Stanton's Units were not subject to Ultrablack, of course, interiorly. It had been the unforeseen darkness in

Stanton's windows that had left Frank in immobile puzzlement on the walk before the Unit.

Seeing Bodger and Grace in the doorway, he turned the wheels of his ponderous vehicle and rolled their way, hoping for information as to Andra's whereabouts. He had just come within a few feet of the twosome, and was about to climb out the back panel when Bodger spoke, hearing the sound of the arriving prop-Goon and thinking it was his requested escort.

"What are you waiting for? We're in a hurry."

Bodger spoke blindly, unable to penetrate the black pall beyond his doorway. Frank hesitated, then decided not to reveal himself as yet. As tonelessly as possible, he spoke to Bodger in the required formula. "Orders."

"You have your orders," Bodger snapped, too keyed up to note any deviation in the accustomed path of the—he assumed—robotic voice. "Take us to Miss Horton's Unit at once."

Frank, believing Stanton was still there, had a chill of apprehension. This man, the Secondary Speakster, might not be on the side of revolt; after all, why should he be? For all he knew, Andra was dead, and Bodger was now on his way back to release the President. The whole business of socking him might have been a blind, to win her confidence, and worm the names of the movement's members from her.

"Do you hear me?" Bodger said, although Frank's worried pause had been barely a moments' duration. "Take us at once. All orders conveyed."

Frank manipulated the arm of the hollow robot up into the doorway, and Bodger, seeing it, took hold. Grace took Bodger's other hand, and then Frank, needing time to think the thing out, turned the bulk of his machine about slowly and began to roll toward the lift. He thought of getting Bodger and the Horton girl out in the toils of Ultrablack and then suddenly deserting them, but hesitated to try it; they might, after all, be what he'd begun to believe they were: sympathetic with the movement.

Their reasons for the return to the girl's Unit might be even Anti-Hive in nature. Frank did not know what to do, so he simply kept moving, got aboard the lift, and thumbed the ninety-three button after Bodger and Grace Horton were safely within the gates.

THE lift dropped smoothly seven levels, then halted, and the gate swung automatically open. And there, his eyes hidden behind a peculiar faceplate, stood Fredric Stanton, hand in hand with Robert Lennick.

"*Bodger!*" Stanton exploded, seeing him through the filter of his face piece. Bodger, hearing the voice in the darkness, drew back into a corner of the lift, staring wide-eyed, futilely, for the other man, trying to hide the slim body of Grace Horton behind him, fearing a repeat of Stanton's attack with the Snapper-Beam.

"Where is he!?" she gasped, terrified by that disembodied, menacing voice in the blackness. Stanton, secure in his invisibility, stepped into the lift, ignoring the metal body of the supposed Goon, and slapped Bodger viciously across the face. While Bodger choked at the unexpected blow, and brought his hand up to his injured mouth, Frank realized there was no longer a doubt where the sympathies of the Secondary Speakster lay, and with one swing of the jointed metal arm of the prop-Goon, he knocked Stanton unconscious with a blow to the base of the skull.

"What happened?" Grace shrilled, clinging to Bodger.

Lennick, deprived of his guide, groped forward in panic, calling, "Mr. Stanton!" Frank spun the controls, and the metal arm swung up and clasped Lennick viciously about the throat, lifting his kicking body clear off the floor.

"Bodger!" Frank called out, enjoying the icy terror that flickered in Lennick's congested face at the sound of his voice. "Stanton's out cold at your feet. He has some sort of face piece he can see with. Put it on!"

Bodger, utterly bewildered as to the sudden turn of events, nevertheless did as directed, and straightened up adjusting the filter over his eyes. When he saw the grisly tableau of Lennick and the prop-Goon, he stepped back, agape with shock. Frank answered his query before Bodger's reeling mind could formulate it coherently. "This is a movie prop. I'm Frank Shawn, a member of Andra's movement, Bodger. And this wriggling worm in my hands is the guy who tried to undo all of us!"

"Frank...please..." Lennick gurgled, his eyes distending while his hands tore vainly at the heavy metal hands that were tightening about his windpipe.

"Let him go," Bodger said impatiently. "He can't get far in Ultrablack, anyhow. We've got to get to Lloyd, my son. He's down at the Brain, now. With Stanton in our power, we can free the Hive forever in an hour's time."

Frank looked at the face of his erstwhile friend, Robert Lennick, and suddenly had no more stomach for murder. He let go, and as Lennick dropped to the floor of the lift and started to double over, gulping air, Frank sent the left arm of the prop-Goon up in an arc that swatted him backwards onto the street outside the gate. Lennick scrambled blindly to his feet, screaming, "Frank! Don't leave me, Frank!" He dashed forward, misjudged his angle, and crashed head-on into a building wall. Frank thumbed the lift-button for Sub-Level One, and let the closing gate blot Lennick from his sight. The lift began to drop, swiftly.

Lennick, after lying painfully on the ground until his addled senses returned, got up on hands and knees, groggily shaking his head. Then, in the darkness, he heard rolling wheels, coming nearer. "Help!" he cried. "This way! Help!"

The rumbling veered in his direction at once, and then a Goon's unseen arms were lifting him to his feet. "The President—" Lennick cried. "He's in danger!"

A moment's hesitance, and the Goon flatly replied, "The President is in no danger. He has been taken to the Brain at his own request, under competent escort."

Lennick, suddenly divining what must be the case, said, "His plate! Someone must have his plate, then, because—"

"You are bleeding," the Goon said dispassionately.

Bob's fingers came up to his face and he winced at the smarting pain their exploration produced at the point where he had struck the building wall. "It's nothing," he said, impatiently. "We've got to—"

"We will take you for hospitalization at once," said the voice of the Goon in the blackness.

"Hospitalization?" Bob said, irritably. "Don't you guys understand? The President—" And then it sank in. *"No!"* he shrieked. *"You can't! I'm on your side!"*

Other sets of heavy wheels rolled nearer, and inflexible metal fingers closed over his arms. The Goons began to roll ponderously off, with Bob firmly in their grasp. He was still shrieking when the mouth of the incinerator chute enveloped him.

LLOYD and Andra were awaiting the lift at Sub-Level one, guided in the blackness by the Goon who had led them to the control chamber, when Bodger and the others arrived. Stanton, only semi-conscious, was being held upright in the arms of the prop-Goon, lest a real Goon pick him up for "treatment" because of his bruises, one on the back of his head where Frank had connected, the other glowing a steadily darker purple on his jaw where Bodger's knockout punch had landed earlier. Lloyd, sensing the tenancy of the lift even in the blackness, drew back apprehensively, and then his father's voice was speaking to him in assurance.

"Whatever orders you've given your guide, son, take them back. We've got you-know-who, and we're taking him to the Brain with us." Andra's fingers closed joyously over Lloyd's own at the words, but he pulled his fingers free and slipped Stanton's Voteplate into his guide's chest-slot.

"Last order countermanded," he said to the Goon. "We have no further need of you. All orders conveyed." The Goon removed the plate, handed it to him, and wheeled off into the darkness. "Dad!" he spoke, then. "I found out so much, from the Brain! The Plan—for reactivating the ten cities—The Brain said you knew where it was."

"Grace will tell you, son," said Bodger. "Meantime—" he pressed Lloyd's own Voteplate into his hand "—take this, you'll need it. And give me Stanton's. I'm taking him down to the Brain. I may have to break his arm for him, but he's going to call off the Goons before I'm through."

"Mr. Bodger—" Frank said, taking out Stanton's preempted Snapper and holding it forward into the darkness. "This may come in handy for persuasion. There's no need to overtax yourself."

Bodger reached out and took it from him. "Thank you, Shawn. Rest assured I'll be only too glad to use it on him if he balks." Bodger motioned to Frank, still in the prop-Goon. "See if you can shake him awake, or something. I don't know how he can get down the ladder except on foot, much as I'd like to drop him into the chamber, if I thought it wouldn't break his rotten neck."

Frank did so, gladly, while Grace, fumbling for and finding Lloyd in the darkness, clung to him in joy and relief. He found himself liking it, and slipped his arms around her to enjoy it the better.

"Frank—" Andra said, slowly, hurt. "We found out, from the Brain, that Bob—Bob's in Stanton's pay."

"We found out, too, Andy," Frank said from inside the pseudo-robot. "The hard way. We left him in Ultrablack on ninety-three. The louse had freed Stanton, and—"

"He's coming to," Bodger said.

IN the agitated shaking of the metal hands that supported him by the upper arms, Stanton blinked wildly at Ultrablack, and choked out, "Let me go! I demand that you release me!"

"You're no longer in a position to demand anything," Bodger said softly. "I have your skinny carcass covered with a Snapper. You may as well relax."

"Bodger...what are you going to do?" Stanton said, no longer fighting the grip of the prop-Goon's hands.

"Take you to the Brain. Make you countermand all your orders regarding the Goons."

"And if I don't?" Stanton said, warily. "What will you do if I refuse?"

"Kill you," Bodger said, and his tone rang true. "I don't want to do it that way, of course...not for reasons of pity; heaven knows you need killing, Fred...but because it's faster this way. With you dead, we'd simply elect a new President, and then he could countermand your orders. That could take days, though, days of the Ultrablack you had Madge Benedict instigate in this emergency. It would be too tedious convincing the Kinsmen to Vote in the dark on a proposition they couldn't see."

"I—" Stanton said blankly, "I thought you'd force Madge to turn on Light-of-Day."

"We would, but Lloyd mistakenly ordered her held incommunicado," Bodger said tiredly. "He didn't know that was another of your pet phrases synonymous with death."

"Good Lord!" Lloyd moaned in the darkness. "I didn't *dream—*"

"Madge brought it on herself, working hand in glove with Stanton, son," Bodger said. "You did not know. The point is, only Stanton or his personal Secretary could have called off the emergency. So now we have to get tough with him."

"Bodger..." Stanton straightened up, his face grim in defeat. "I have to know: If I do as you ask—countermand the Goons, call off the Ultrablack—what will happen to me, afterwards?"

"I can't say, Fred," Bodger replied flatly. "We'll have it put to a general Vote."

"I see," said the President, knowing full well what the result of such a Vote would be, with the Hive enraged against his exposed treachery. "Is it your best offer?"

"My only," said Bodger, "Let's go, Fred."

He prodded Stanton's back with the Snapper, and the President began to move forward, holding his head high, toward the staircase leading to the control chamber entrance. Frank opened the panel at the rear of the prop-Goon, and called for Andra to join him inside it, then he took Lloyd and Grace by the arms, via the controls, and guided them through the black blindness after Bodger and his prisoner.

AT the head of the staircase—really no more than a tier-cut segment of the lead-concrete Sub-Level Two, over which the correspondingly undercut left wall of the twenty-five-foot-thick level could slide—Frank had to come to a halt, his prop-Goon not being equipped with extendable cogs to fit the treads and risers, as the real Goons' wheels were. "I'm going down there with him," Lloyd said, starting down into blackness.

"No," his father's voice came from the level below. "I'll handle this myself, Lloyd. I can see my way and you can't."

Lloyd stood undecided on the brink of the staircase, then Grace found his arm in the dark and drew him back. "I want to talk to you about your father, Lloyd," she said, when he was again at her side. "He said some strange things, up in the Unit..."

Descending the ladder below his prisoner, the Snapper aimed upward always at the base of Stanton's spine, Bodger reached the cable-net flooring, and gestured the President to the chair before the control panel. "Here," he said, returning the other's Voteplate. "You'll need this. But I don't have to tell you the penalty for one attempt at trickery on your part."

Stanton took the card silently, and slid it into a slot on the control panel. A metal square slid back, exposing a hand microphone. He took it in his hand, and spoke into it.

"Primal Speakster in control," he said.

All about the two men, the lights of the Brain flickered then a speaker in the cavity which had held the microphone said, in the cold, flat tones of the Brain, "Orders."

Stanton glanced up at Bodger, and smiled. And suddenly Bodger was afraid. There was no hint of fear in the other man's eyes, now, only confidence and terrible menace.

"There is a false robot, two men and two women with it, on Sub-Level One," said Stanton, while Bodger goggled in surprise. "Destroy them!"

"Orders," said the Brain.

"Stanton!" Bodger raged, snapping out of his stunned paralysis. He depressed the stud of the Snapper clear into the hilt of the weapon, trying to prevent the activating words from being spoken by the President. There was a fractional hum of power, and then a searing fork of hot blue light leaped from a conic protrusion on the Brain's inner surface and turned the weapon to molten metal in his fingers. Bodger fell to the flooring, crying out in pain, his raw, blistered hand nearly driving him unconscious.

"You should have known," Stanton addressed the mewling figure on the ground near his chair, "that a sonic beam cannot be fired inside the Brain; it would shatter some of the delicate balances necessary for its functioning. The Brain has to safeguard itself."

"*Stanton*—" Bodger groaned, gritting his teeth against the agony of his seared hand. "Don't! Please..."

"Danger," said the dispassionate voice of the Brain.

STANTON spun to face the concavity of the speaker. "What—?" he blurted, baffled. And then he heard the dim rumble, high above, as the entire lead-concrete Sub-Level Two slid relentlessly closed. Stanton jumped from the chair and looked up from the base of the ladder, to see if his ears had told him the truth. All that was visible at the head of the hundred-foot ladder was the bottom of the now-closed metal lid, over which the entire next level had moved. He turned, white-faced, to Bodger.

"What's happening?"

"*Danger,*" repeated the Brain. Stanton rushed to the side of the fallen man. "Bodger!" he shrieked, lifting him by the shoulders and shaking him. "What's happening!?"

"I guess—" Bodger said, smiling tiredly despite the cruel burns, "—I must've got mad, Fred. My innards, or don't you know about them?"

"I know all about your radiating innards!" Stanton exploded. "But *they* couldn't trigger the Brain's protective level! It's impossible! You've been here before—"

"I was never...this aroused...before, Fred," Bodger said weakly. "And now, for the first time, I...know the answer to something. I never knew before." He took a breath, gathered together all his strength, and lifted his face near the other man's, still smiling. "You asked the Brain about a third term, once. - Don't argue, Fred, it's on record—and yet there is no memory in its circuits of a reply. Tell me, Fred...what was its reply?" When Stanton did not respond, Bodger said, "I think I can tell you. Chaos. Noise. A riot of sound and fury that knocked you clear off your chair and broke the circuit before it destroyed you. Because the Brain knew, of course. It's smart, Fred. It can predict with better accuracy than a human mind. It foresaw, after correlating all the facts at its disposal, what would be the result of your attempt at being elected a third time. And it tried to...tell you..." Bodger faltered, went gray, and lay back upon the interwoven cables with his eyes closed. His lips were still working, though, and he finished, "...the result...except that the...Brain doesn't speak...in words...just concepts...and its concept encompassed...its own..."

His head rolled to one side, limply.

"Danger," croaked the voice of the Brain.

"Its *what?* Its own *what!?*" Stanton yelled, grabbing Bodger's head by the hair and banging it violently upon the flooring. Bodger, his eyes rolling, coughed painfully, then sighed, as one who names a long-awaited friend, "...death."

"Danger!" said the Brain. A wild tootling began in its depths as its metal mind tried to spare it its terrible fate.

"What danger?" Stanton roared into the microphone, leaping to the chair before the control panel. "Tell me! I'll find a way out!"

"Danger!" said the Brain. *"Danger! Danger!"*

There was a wild bluish light playing on the face of the panel, now, and Stanton knew, suddenly, that it was not of the Brain itself. He turned, some hideous psychic insight telling him what he could not as yet realize by his senses, and looked at the body of Lloyd Bodger on the floor.

Veins and arteries shone like a network of neon lights through the flesh, a pulsing glow that rose in its intensity by the second. The internal organs appeared through Bodger's smoldering clothing as on the screen of a fluoroscope, each alight with self-engendered hellfire. Bodger's eyes were glowing like hot tungsten through his transparent lids, his teeth were bared in a smile brighter than sunrise. His every bone, bit of cartilage, nerve ganglion and muscle fiber sparked like coals beneath a blacksmith's bellows, and the hairs of his head were a Medusa-wig of burning, writhing wire.

And then he reached his critical mass.

THE END

If you've enjoyed this book, you will not want to miss these terrific titles...

ARMCHAIR SCI-FI & HORROR DOUBLE NOVELS, $12.95 each

D-1 **THE GALAXY RAIDERS** by William P. McGivern
SPACE STATION #1 by Frank Belknap Long

D-2 **THE PROGRAMMED PEOPLE** by Jack Sharkey
SLAVES OF THE CRYSTAL BRAIN by William Carter Sawtelle

D-3 **YOU'RE ALL ALONE** by Fritz Leiber
THE LIQUID MAN by Bernard C. Gilford

D-4 **CITADEL OF THE STAR LORDS** by Edmond Hamilton
VOYAGE TO ETERNITY by Milton Lesser

D-5 **IRON MEN OF VENUS** by Don Wilcox
THE MAN WITH ABSOLUTE MOTION by Noel Loomis

D-6 **WHO SOWS THE WIND...** by Rog Phillips
THE PUZZLE PLANET by Robert A. W. Lowndes

D-7 **PLANET OF DREAD** by Murray Leinster
TWICE UPON A TIME by Charles L. Fontenay

D-8 **THE TERROR OUT OF SPACE** by Dwight V. Swain
QUEST OF THE GOLDEN APE by Ivar Jorgensen and Adam Chase

D-9 **SECRET OF MARRACOTT DEEP** by Henry Slesar
PAWN OF THE BLACK FLEET by Mark Clifton.

D-10 **BEYOND THE RINGS OF SATURN** by Robert Moore Williams
A MAN OBSESSED by Alan E. Nourse

ARMCHAIR SCIENCE FICTION CLASSICS, $12.95 each

C-1 **THE GREEN MAN**
by Harold M. Sherman

C-2 **A TRACE OF MEMORY**
By Keith Laumer

C-3 **INTO PLUTONIAN DEPTHS**
by Stanton A. Coblentz

ARMCHAIR MASTERS OF SCIENCE FICTION SERIES, $16.95 each

M-1 **MASTERS OF SCIENCE FICTION, Vol. One**
Bryce Walton—"Dark of the Moon" and other tales

M-2 **MASTERS OF SCIENCE FICTION, Vol. Two**
Jerome Bixby—"One Way Street" and other tales

If you've enjoyed this book, you will not want to miss these terrific titles…

ARMCHAIR SCI-FI & HORROR DOUBLE NOVELS, $12.95 each

D-11　**PERIL OF THE STARMEN** by Kris Neville
THE STRANGE INVASION by Murray Leinster

D-12　**THE STAR LORD** by Boyd Ellanby
CAPTIVES OF THE FLAME by Samuel R. Delany

D-13　**MEN OF THE MORNING STAR** by Edmond Hamilton
PLANET FOR PLUNDER by Hal Clement and Sam Merwin, Jr.

D-14　**ICE CITY OF THE GORGON** by Chester S. Geier and Richard Shaver
WHEN THE WORLD TOTTERED by Lester del Rey

D-15　**WORLDS WITHOUT END** by Clifford D. Simak
THE LAVENDER VINE OF DEATH by Don Wilcox

D-16　**SHADOW ON THE MOON** by Joe Gibson
ARMAGEDDON EARTH by Geoff St. Reynard

D-17　**THE GIRL WHO LOVED DEATH** by Paul W. Fairman
SLAVE PLANET by Laurence M. Janifer

D-18　**SECOND CHANCE** by J. F. Bone
MISSION TO A DISTANT STAR by Frank Belknap Long

D-19　**THE SYNDIC** by C. M. Kornbluth
FLIGHT TO FOREVER by Poul Anderson

D-20　**SOMEWHERE I'LL FIND YOU** by Milton Lesser
THE TIME ARMADA by Fox B. Holden

ARMCHAIR SCIENCE FICTION CLASSICS, $12.95 each

C-4　**CORPUS EARTHLING**
by Louis Charbonneau

C-5　**THE TIME DISSOLVER**
by Jerry Sohl

C-6　**WEST OF THE SUN**
by Edgar Pangborn

ARMCHAIR SCI-FI & HORROR GEMS SERIES, $12.95 each

G-1　**SCIENCE FICTION GEMS, Vol. One**
Isaac Asimov and others

G-2　**HORROR GEMS, Vol. One**
Carl Jacobi and others

BEWARE...THE MECHANICAL BRAINIAC!

It was almost too terrifying to think about. Thankfully, most of humanity knew nothing of its existence; but hidden somewhere in the bowels of the city was a horrible menace—a mechanical menace whose real purpose was decidedly evil.

Joe January was a hard-boiled government man who became one of the unlucky few to gain knowledge of this cerebral monstrosity. He and the others feared for their lives and trembled at the thought of it. For he knew that unless a way could be found to destroy it, the future of mankind was in great peril. Yet there was an even darker horror that lurked beyond. Ever hear of a "penth?" You will soon enough, in this chilling classic from the golden age of science fiction, written by Hugo nominee, Rog Phillips, writing as William Carter Sawtelle.

CAST OF CHARACTERS

JOE JANUARY
An agent of the government, he was the first to encounter the horror of the Crystal Brain and come back alive.

NANCY HOWARD
She worked faithfully for one of the world's most powerful men, but what was the secret she guarded so carefully?

GILES LORTON
He used his great power and wealth for a horrible purpose—one that threatened to destroy the entire world.

DR. ATKINSON
This kindly scientist found out—in the most horrifying way imaginable—that too much knowledge can be a dangerous thing.

WISHWELL
A great scientist, he worked feverishly on the one weapon that could save mankind.

GRAY SUIT
Outwardly he appeared to be a loyal slave of the Crystal Brain...or was he?

THE CRYSTAL BRAIN
This mechanical monstrosity threatened to control the entire world—but what controlled it?

SLAVES OF THE CRYSTAL BRAIN

By
WILLIAM CARTER SAWTELLE
(aka Rog Phillips)

ARMCHAIR FICTION
PO Box 4369, Medford, Oregon 97504

CHAPTER ONE

"ROUTINE check, sir," January called out as he shoved open the lab door. He didn't knock. In his business and under these circumstances, a knock or any other intimation that he was coming was not only undesirable but was strictly against the rules. Members of the checking staff of the FSB—Federal Security Bureau—came down like the Assyrians of old, as wolves upon the fold, their purpose to count lambs.

Going through the door, he stepped into the brightest laboratory he had ever seen. From the ceiling a whole bank of lights poured down hundreds of watts of electric current transformed into light. Small but powerful floodlights illuminated each corner of the room. In addition, floor lamps shed a brilliant luster upward.

The second he saw the lights, he guessed that the man in this lab was scared of the dark.

It was a new development. He had checked Dr. Atkinson in this lab not two months previously. The lights had not been here then.

"Federal Security, sir," he spoke to the big man crouching over the battered desk in the middle of the littered laboratory. "Routine check. How are you, Dr. Atkinson?" He grinned when he spoke and the grin took a little of the wary alertness off his lean brown face.

"Damn it!" Until January spoke the second time, Atkinson had not realized he had a visitor. He turned a great thatch of white hair and a startled angry face toward the intruder. For an instant, living fear gleamed in his eyes. Then he recognized January. "Oh, it's you, is it? Get the hell out. I'm busy."

SLAVES of the

Hidden somwhere from the eyes of man was a machine with an evil purpose; yet even its worst enemies protected it

It seemed to January that the globe feared light even more than bullets. But on it came

January did not move. "Sorry, sir," he said.

Atkinson's face changed. "It is I who should be apologizing

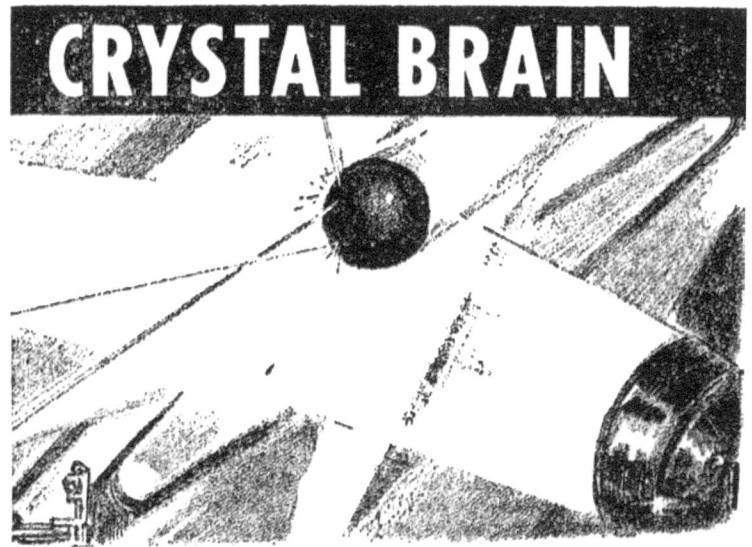

CRYSTAL BRAIN

By William Carter Sawtelle

rather than you. You have your duty. I could at least be pleasant about it, since it's for my own protection, but the truth is—I—I was thinking."

"It's quite all right, sir," January answered. His face had lost none of its pleasant good nature. He was accustomed to the way scientists reacted to him. Most of them didn't like the intrusions of the FSB men and plainly said so. The best of them accepted the checkers grudgingly, as just another evil some damned bureaucrat had thought up to hamper the work of honest men. There was nothing personal involved, personally most of them seemed to like this tall lean man whose face never lost its smile—nor its wary alertness—it was just that scientists somehow could not accustom themselves to the idea that they were important enough for anybody to care whether they were alive or not. Their work was important; to a man they thought the particular job each was doing was the most important bit of research ever undertaken on the top side of the earth or planned for the far side of the moon, but they themselves were not important.

JANUARY watched the anger and the irritation and the intrusion go out of the scientist's eyes. But the fear did not go. Casually Atkinson closed his desk drawer. "But I still say you ought to give fair warning when you are coming."

"We can't," the agent answered. "It's like a sentry walking a beat. Anybody who wants to get past the sentry first checks his routing and determines where the sentry will be. Then, when the sentry is somewhere else, the intruder walks past. The FSB doesn't operate according to routine. I am checking you now. I may be back to check you early in the morning. Or somebody else may be here tomorrow. On the other hand, no agent may visit you for the next month. That way, it will be a little harder for anybody to kidnap you."

"Now who in hell would be kidnapping me?" the scientist asked. A sudden wariness crept into his voice.

January laid his briefcase on the desk and unlocked it. "I don't know. But Preston and Howe are still missing."

Behind the desk, Atkinson was suddenly silent. Evasively silent, January thought. He began to take the equipment out of his brief case.

In February, 1970, James Ward Preston, a prominent physicist, had vanished. The fact that he was even missing had not been known for weeks. By the time it was discovered, the trail had grown cold, any clues that might have been left behind vanished.

One missing scientist might not have caused a furore. He might have suffered an attack of amnesia, any of a dozen things might have happened to him. It was not too important. A month later, it became more important.

William Henry Howe, a brilliant theoretical mathematician, also vanished.

Right then and there the FSB had been created. Its purpose was simple—to check constantly on every important scientist in America, to make certain all were present and accounted for. After all was said and done, the real strength of a nation rested not on its stockpile of atom bombs, not in its steel and coal industries, but in its supply of brains. If two top-flight scientists could disappear and leave behind no trace of what had happened, why couldn't twenty go the same way?

What had happened to Preston and Howe? Nobody knew. If the void had opened and had swallowed them, they could not have vanished more completely.

Was the European Federation kidnapping American scientists? No one who knew the real facts of the world situation ever quite believed this was true but it didn't cost much to send somebody around every week or two to every top-flight scientist to make certain he was still alive and still on the job, whatever his job was.

At first the scientists had been highly indignant, yelling that their personal privacy was being invaded and that the irregular visits of the security men interfered with their work; then their attitude had become one of patient resignation: as you accepted rain and mud, you accepted security men. After all, they didn't take up too much of your valuable time, they just checked your fingerprints to make certain they had the right man, they inquired politely into your health and how you were feeling and had you seen anything suspicious? And it was sort of flattering to know that the government thought you were so important. After you got over being irritated, you were just a little pleased, especially since the FSB men were invariably good people.

"Bosh!" Atkinson said. "Preston and Howe were no more kidnapped that I am likely to be—" He caught himself in mid-sentence. His gaze came quickly up to January's face, to see if the FSB men had paid any attention to what had been said.

JANUARY, still taking equipment out of his briefcase, seemed not to be listening. As Atkinson stopped speaking, a feeling of cold appeared out of nowhere, charging deep centers of the agent's mind. He thought: this man is afraid of something more definite than the dark. For an instant, he tried to let his mind explore the meaning and the nature of the fear he sensed here, then shrugged the thought aside. This was a routine inspection. It was his job to determine if the man sitting at the desk was actually William B. Atkinson, Ph.D., and to ask said individual if he had anything to say. That was all there was to it.

January had made hundreds of such inspections and nothing had ever happened—yet. Atkinson had been visited dozens of times. Without being asked, the scientist extended his right hand. January took the thumbprint on a square of transparent plastic, slipped it into the comparison viewer. As he brought the viewer to his eyes, he was aware that the scientist was watching him with the wariness of a crouching rabbit that suspects the presence of a wolf. A thin film of sweat was visible on Atkinson's forehead.

The prints matched. This man was Atkinson. January took the viewer from his eyes. "I see you have cut your finger," he said. The print had revealed a new scratch on the thumb.

"Yes. Last week." Atkinson obviously did not have his mind on what he was saying. He had picked up a pencil and was making apparently meaningless marks on a piece of paper. "Chunk of glass. Did you catch the scar on the print?"

"Yes." According to the rules, this interview was over. January ought to be leaving. But he hesitated. "Anything you want to say, sir?"

"No." There was hesitation in the voice.

"Has anything that you regard as suspicious happened since the last security agent visited you?"

"N-o." Atkinson looked up from the paper. His hand was shaking. The sweat had spread from his forehead to his whole face. His eyes went round the laboratory, searching, for something, then came back to the paper on his desk. January looked at the paper. Doodles filled the white sheet, hen tracks, a house with smoke coming out of the chimney, trees, a dog. The agent blinked, looked again to make sure. His gaze froze on the sheet of paper.

Spread through the doodles were the words—*I know what happened to Howe.*

January's eyes jerked up to Atkinson's face. The film of sweat had spread. Globules of yellow perspiration glistened on the scientist's skin. Again his eyes went over the brilliantly lighted laboratory, repeating his endless, wary, frightened search for something that he was afraid might be there, something which could perhaps be kept away by intense light. Atkinson wiped at the sweat. "Hot tonight," he said. "Humidity's bad. Sit down, Mr. January. Too hot to work. What do you think of the Cub's chances of winning the pennant this year?"

January slid into the chair beside the desk. Like a private watchman making his rounds, Atkinson's eyes went over the laboratory again.

"If their pitching holds up, they ought to be in," January said. "That Memmeldorff is really some pitcher. Did you see the game he pitched against the Cards last week?"

"No. Couldn't get away, unfortunately. Too busy." Atkinson tried to grin. The effort failed. He opened the top drawer of his desk an inch, glanced at something inside.

HIS PULSES jumping, January watched. In his day, he had seen a lot of frightened men, criminals fresh caught with the fear of the law still a living yellow color on their faces, men walking toward the death house, knowing what waited for them beyond the green door, men fatally injured in auto and helicopter accidents, knowing what had happened to them and trying to face fearlessly the last final fearful act of every man, dying itself. He had seen the crash of Rocket II, the second passenger-carrying rocket to try for the moon. Forty miles up, something had gone wrong with the ship's steering equipment. Rocket II had turned in a circle and at full speed had dived nose first into the Chaco Desert, the fuel tanks blowing when the ship hit. The remains had not been fear inspiring in themselves, not enough had been left to make even a bad smell, but January, inspecting those remains, had had no trouble in imagining the feelings of the poor devils who had ridden the ship down.

It struck January that Atkinson was nearly the most frightened man he had ever seen. Scientists usually had an odd lot of fear complexes. The evils that most men feared, depression, loss of job, loss of health, even death itself, did not seem to impress most scientists as cause for fear. These evils, these dangers, they ignored. But they were afraid just the same, down to the last man they were afraid—of the facts and of the possibilities that their science was opening up for them, of the awesome depths of nature they were exploring.

For centuries past the counting the human race had been exploring nature. Primitive magic has been an attempt to explore and to control the strong, vital forces that men felt were in existence around them. Unless there was more truth than had ever been revealed, sorcery and magic had not been adequate exploratory or control tools. Science was a much better tool. Maybe it was too good.

As they used this tool to explore the universe, the

scientists seemed to act as if the things they saw with their microscopes and their telescopes frightened them. Always January had had the impression that the scientists were wondering about some mysterious entity that existed just beyond the range of the biggest telescope, the best electron microscope, some vast, hidden, primal something for which they had no name but which they were afraid they would someday rouse to wakefulness, with disastrous results, much as a hunter rouses a hibernating bear—and wishes to hell he had left the monster sound asleep.

Perhaps something that would sweep the human race from existence, that would take over this green planet, something against which man and the science of man could not compete.

This, the scientists seemed to fear.

From the desk drawer, Atkinson cautiously took a small cardboard box. Sticking through a slit in the top of the box was what looked like a crude, hand-made finger ring, set with a small red stone that was dull and lifeless. Atkinson lifted the pencil again. Mixed among the doodles were the words:

"If that stone begins to glow, talk about baseball."

January nodded. In the back of his mind was the thought, *has this man gone insane?* The idea received support when the scientist got up and moved across the lab, switching on additional lights, making the brightness almost intolerable.

"It doesn't like light, that I know," Atkinson spoke, his voice a whisper. "Maybe light will protect us. Maybe. Some vibratory frequency will protect us. But which frequency?" He seemed to muse over a long-considered problem.

"Protect us from what?" January spoke.

"I think it's all right to talk, but it is safest to whisper," Atkinson answered. "From a *penth*."

"What?"

ATKINSON seemed not to hear him. Again the man was staring around the laboratory, again he was listening. Sweat was making tiny rivulets down his face. January felt the creep of cold. Atkinson slipped back into the chair at his desk. "I have seen Howe," he whispered.

"You have seen Howe?" January repeated the words carefully.

"Yes. But Michaelson made the original discovery, January. You know who he is. Or you can find out. Michaelson is your starting point—" He broke off. His gaze came to rest on the ring sitting on the desk in front of him.

Like a warning light in the fog, the stone in the setting had begun to glow blood red.

Coming from nowhere and from everywhere, from the walls, from the ceiling, from the floors, from the very air itself, was a thin weird mechanical voice.

"At-kin-son. At-kin-son."

A strangled cry forming in his throat, the scientist leaped to his feet. His eyes darted around the room, came to rest on a spot directly above his head. January followed the line of the scientist's gaze. His first dazed impression was that his eyes were deceiving him.

Up near the ceiling, where the lights poured in a brilliant flood, a shadow was forming.

Where no shadow could possibly exist, a shadow was coming into existence.

It was growing larger. In the split second while January watched, the shadow swirled with increasing blackness, and became a blob of darkness the size of a doubled fist.

It was the blackest thing January had ever seen. Beside it, ebony was a shade of gray. In comparison to this total darkness, the heart of midnight was like the bright light of a summer afternoon. Where the human eye, registering the absence of all light, calls an object black, the blackness of this thing was not only the absence of light, it was the absence of anything.

Where nothing exists there is no light.

This thing was nothing.

In an instant, it had formed and had enlarged to the size of a toy balloon. As Atkinson, dry husky croaks sounding in his throat, jerked open the door of his desk and pawed frantically for something in there, it began to move toward him, moving sluggishly as if it did not relish the blaze of light in this room, or was somehow impeded by the existence of the light, but moving just the same.

The laboratory echoed to the roar of thunder as the FSB agent snatched the gun holstered under his left shoulder and pulled the trigger. January was hardly conscious of his action. Intuitively as he recognized the blob of darkness as a source of danger, subconscious reflex actions took care of pulling the gun.

The bullets struck the target. He could not see them strike it but he could see a swirl in the blob of darkness each time he pulled the trigger.

The bullets did not go through the ball; they did not strike the ceiling above. They also had no affect whatsoever on the ball of darkness, did not in the least slow its progress.

January stared at the gun in his hand. It was a compact but very powerful weapon. It would literally stop the charge of an elephant. But it did not stop the advance of this thing.

"At-kin-son. At-kin-son." Again the shrill whisper sounded in the room. There was a mechanical note about the voice, each syllable was carefully pronounced, there was absolutely no accent.

"Damn you!" The scientist snatched something from his desk. It was a little weapon of some kind. He pointed the weapon upward. From it jutted a beam of light.

January flinched involuntarily. The light was so bright as

to be blinding, to hurt the eyes. Atkinson had taken refuge in a brightly lighted laboratory. Now he was trying to use a weapon of light.

From between slitted lids, the FSB agent saw the light beam hit the ball of blackness. Bullets had not stopped it. Nor did the beam of light. It rolled to one side, dodging the light, and kept coming.

"Run, January," Atkinson yelled. "This is a *penth!*"

FEAR IN shocking waves of biting cold rolled over the FSB agent but he did not run. Men who worked for the FSB were selected with the idea in mind that they would not run. Every impulse in Joe January shrieked to him to run. He moved forward.

"Stay away from me!" Atkinson shouted. Simultaneously the light from the weapon began to falter. The *penth* moved rapidly forward.

Atkinson must have known then how the struggle was going to end. "Check on Michaelson, January." Check so far as he got—but no farther. The *penth* touched his arm.

He screamed.

Where it touched his arm, the arm vanished. From his right hand, the light weapon dropped to the top of the desk, slid from the desk to the floor.

Atkinson turned a tortured face toward January. "*Penth* from the Crystal Brain—" The *penth* flowed up his left arm. He tried to shake it off; it clung like a leech. As it moved upward, nothing was left behind it. It rolled over his shoulder. He screamed then, for the last time. The blackness folded over his head. Like a river of ink running downhill, it flowed over his body.

Nothing was left behind.

It raced downward to the floor. For an instant, to January's horror-struck eyes, it seemed to linger an inch or two above the floor. As it hung there, a whisper of distant laughter seemed to echo through the room.

Then it vanished.

As it disappeared, the tiny red jewel in the setting of the ring on the desk ceased to glow.

Where a man had stood a minute before, now there was nothing.

Waves of living cold washed over the body of Joe January. He felt his hair rise. Every impulse in his body shrieked to him to run—somewhere, anywhere, it didn't matter where, just so he got away from this place. His lips moved, forming words.

"Atkinson. Atkinson…" he whispered.

There was no answer. He knew there wouldn't be. With his own eyes, he had seen Atkinson vanish; he had watched - the scientist go away as no other mortal had ever gone before, so far as he knew.

So far as he knew!

Preston and Howe had gone. Atkinson had said that he knew what had happened to Howe. Had Preston and Howe gone the same way Atkinson had gone, like rabbits disappearing down the gullet of a snake? At the thought, the agent felt his skin creep.

What was this thing that Atkinson had called a *penth* and had come out of nowhere to devour him? Was devour the word to describe what had happened? January had had the impression that the *penth* was feeding, though perhaps he had been mistaken in that. Perhaps some other process was in action. His sense impressions told him that Atkinson had been devoured but in the state of shock in which he knew himself to be, his sense impressions were not trustworthy.

He concentrated every effort of his will on one simple task, reaching into the pocket of his coat for a package of cigarettes. He had to try three times before he could get a cigarette out of the package. Then he broke it. He got the second one to his lips and bit into it as if it were a cigar.

"Damn you, Joe January...get control of yourself!"

He spat out crumbs of tobacco and pieces of paper. The next cigarette was accepted by his lips. He broke two matches before he got one lit, then the third match went out before he could get it to the cigarette. Again he cursed himself. The next time he tried, he succeeded in lighting the cigarette.

In this one fact, he knew he had achieved a major psychic victory. He had himself under control.

Without moving from the spot where he stood, he reached out a hand for the phone on Atkinson's desk. The number he dialed was not in any phone book. It was a direct long-distance connection. Even he did not know where the phone he was calling was located—it might be in Toledo, St. Louis, here in Chicago—but the person who answered it would consider the call an emergency and would relay instantly to the chief of the FSB every word January reported.

Before he had finished dialing, the stone setting on the ring had begun to glow.

He looked at it, somberly, considering the various things this one fact could mean.

No matter what it meant, he knew he didn't like it. Very cautiously and carefully, he replaced the phone and looked around the laboratory for whatever was to be seen there.

CHAPTER TWO

WORKING LATE, the girl was busy transcribing letters. The other five girls in the office had gone home but she had volunteered to remain and finish up all dictation for the day. It was nothing unusual for her to do this. Of all the employees of Giles Lorton, Inc., Nancy Howard was the most faithful and the most willing worker. Since she had come to work in this office three months before, she had not been late a single time and she had not missed a day.

Her fingers flowed over the keys of the electric typewriter as she took Mr. Lorton's dictation from the wire recording. The switch that controlled the operation of the recorder was located under her desk, where the pressure of her toe could turn it on or off. She was a competent, but not expert, typist; consequently, there were frequent mis-hit keys or strikeovers, necessitating the use of an eraser. But each misspelled word and each typographical error was carefully, competently, and completely erased and corrected and the letters were perfect before she took them in to Mr. Lorton for his signature. If the recording was not clear, she ran the wire over and over again until the doubtful word was certain, listening to the voice in the earphones with her head cocked to one side like some perplexed and slightly puzzled wren.

In fact, she wasn't much bigger than a wren, but she was very well developed. Nancy Howard was an NPN girl. NPN—No Padding Necessary.

The building in which she worked was located on Michigan Avenue, Chicago 1, Illinois. You entered this building through one of many solid glass doors set in polished aluminum that looked like platinum and probably cost almost as much, and you found yourself in a marble-floored foyer big enough to contain a working fountain and a statue of cupid, with room enough left over for a platoon to practice all the marching formations they could learn on a parade ground. It was quite an impressive foyer. Banks of almost noiseless elevators whisked people upward and out of sight into mysterious upper regions. There was even a private elevator, but you had to have a special key to enter and operate it. If you had such a key, you could get into this elevator and punch a button and zoom straight up to the roof, where the cage, with a discrete *whoosh*, would deposit you in the elaborate private offices of the man who owned the building.

It was quite an impressive building. Just looking at it, you thought instantly of respectability and refinement. Nothing illegal could ever occur in this building, nothing immoral could happen here, nothing wrong could take place in these sacred premises.

Mr. Lorton would not tolerate any of those things in this place.

Mr. Lorton owned the building.

In his way, Mr. Lorton was one of the big shots in Chicago. Over on LaSalle Street, they regarded him as a financial wizard. His deals always came out right. If he bought a stock, that stock went up. If he sold a stock, that stock was due to take a nosedive. He worked the same way in the grain market.

Yet, oddly, not much was really known about him. He had been in Chicago less than two years. No one knew where he had come from, he never spoke of his past; apparently he had not been rich when he first arrived in town. But he was rich now. That much was certain. Wise people, hoping to make a profit from a deal with him, did not inquire into the sources of his wealth. It was enough to say that he was a financial wizard who had gotten rich in the market. There was no point in asking questions about Giles Lorton, the man, where he had been born, where he had gone to school, *if* he had gone to school—and his speech sometimes indicated a lack of formal education, who his parents were, had one of his ancestors come over on the Mayflower, etc. Giles Lorton, the man, nobody knew. Nobody really cared much. He was rich. So what? Chicago, having seen more millionaires that it can remember, is not inclined to pay too much attention to the breed. Wealth alone is not enough to distinguish any man. Giles Lorton was wealthy but he was otherwise undistinguished—carefully so. Or at least so far as the world in general knew.

Of the people who knew him, perhaps Nancy Howard knew the most about him. Some of her information she had gathered from his dictation—innocuous stuff, strictly, about contracts and agreements and leases and buying and selling and taxes, but still personal enough to reveal something about the man. The majority of her information, however, she had gotten in a way that would have surprised the hell out of him, if he had known about it.

CONCEALED IN the desk of his private office was a miniature radio transmitter. A tiny thing hardly bigger than a thimble, it represented the ultimate in radio design possible to the advanced technology of the year 1972. Developments during World War II, in which a complete radar set had been mounted in the nose of a .90-millimeter shell, resulting in the famous proximity fuse, had paved the way for this thimble-size transmitter. The range of the transmitter in Lorton's private office was not over fifty feet—the high frequency radiations dampened out rapidly—but even this short range was entirely adequate to activate the equally tiny receiver hidden inside the transcriber. Concealed wires ran up the transcriber tubes to a miniature earphone hidden inside the left earplug.

While transcribing dictation, she could also listen to every sound from Lorton's office. If a word was spoken behind those thick oak doors inscribed with the name Mr. Lorton, in those soundproofed premises, it was instantly transmitted to her in the outer office. True, if the transcriber was in operation she also heard the words coming from it, with the result that she could not distinguish between the two, but to correct this deficiency all she had to do was to touch the transcriber cut-off button with her toe, after which the words from the radio came through clear and undistorted.

Of course, while she was listening to the radio, it was wise to be correcting a typographical error at the same time or to pretend to be trying to distinguish a not quite clear word from the transcriber. Anyone watching her would reach the obvious conclusion that she was merely an inexpert typist having trouble with her transcribing, which was true.

She was an inexpert typist.

As to what she was, in addition to being a not quite perfect stenographer, was her secret, and one that she fervidly hoped she would be able to keep as long as was necessary.

As to why she was listening to everything that happened in Mr. Lorton's office, this was also her secret.

Usually Mr. Lorton was in his office from seven until nine each evening. He was not much in evidence during the day and no one knew or cared where he went after he left at nine but he spent two hours in his private sanctum almost every day.

While he was in his office, he talked to someone.

Nancy Howard did not know whom he talked to. It was not a telephone conversation, the telephone switchboard she handled after office hours, it was not a visitor who came in through the regular entrance from the private elevator. There was a second entrance and exit to Mr. Lorton's office, through a door that opened into a corridor served by one of the regular elevators, but Nancy did not think that Mr. Lorton's visitor came this way. She did not think he even had a visitor, she thought he was talking to someone who was somewhere else.

As to how that conversation was transmitted, she did not know. There was no permanent private radio installation in his office; she had searched carefully before she had hidden her own tiny transmitter in his desk. The only conclusion she could reach was that he carried with him a miniature radio transmitter and receiver of his own. This solution was possible. She thought it was probable.

This left unanswered, however, the question of the identity of the person with whom he carried on his private talks.

It was the answer to this question that made her sit on the edge of her chair with her head cocked to one side like a puzzled and badly frightened wren trying to decide if that long straight object in the grass is a stick or a snake.

She didn't think he talked to a *person*.

She thought he talked to a *thing*.

FOR ALL SHE knew, he might not be talking over a radio transmitter at all. No transmitter might be needed. The thing might be right there in the office with him. They might be talking face to face, one on each side of the acres-wide mahogany desk. The thing might be sitting on the desk itself. When Lorton left the office, the thing might go with him, invisible and unseen by anybody else.

Two facts were certain. The thing reported information to him, often seemingly describing events that were taking place miles away. It also took orders from him.

She had heard him issue those orders more than once, in a crisp commanding tone of voice, such orders as: "Report on Number 71."

After a few seconds of silence back would come the answer, in a clicking, metallic, mechanical voice: "Num-ber sev-en one is tak-ing a bath, sir." Or the answer might be that Number 71 was working in the laboratory, or was taking a ride along the Outer Drive, drinking coffee, fighting with his wife, was out with a woman, anything.

Always the report was by number, never by name. She had never heard a name mentioned. A name was one thing she wanted. A name would give her a starting point.

She could not investigate Number 71 or Number 28 or any other number until she knew the name that went along with the number.

Sitting in his office, Lorton could seemingly find out what any of almost a hundred people were doing. He could also tell these people to stop what they were doing or to do something else. They seemed to obey him. From this fact, she had the grim suspicion that he had some way of seeing that his orders were carried out.

She did not know how he gained control of the people who obeyed him or how he forced them to carry out his commands. There were a million things she did not know, it seemed to her, but one fact was crystal clear to her—that she was playing a dangerous and a deadly game. If Lorton ever discovered who she was or that she was spying on him—the very thought sent a wave of terror through her.

But, whatever the risk, she knew she was going to take it.

In her left earphone the whistle that preceded the mechanical voice sounded.

With her toe, she kicked off the transcriber and bent to erase a nonexistent typographical error.

"What is it?" Lorton's voice came.

"Num-ber ni-ne had just been contact-ed by an F S B man."

Nancy Howard did not know what the FSB was or even

that it existed. Few people did. An essential part of the function of the FSB was to stay out of sight and out of knowledge. Apparently, Lorton was one of the few people who did know. She heard him growl a curse.

"Those nosey meddlers."

"Yes, sir."

There was a moment of silence. She had never heard Number 9 mentioned before. Apparently Lorton had forgotten his identity. "Who is Number Nine? I seem to have forgotten."

Bent over her typewriter, Nancy Howard held her breath.

"At-kin-son," the mechanical voice came. "William B. At-kin-son. PHD. Res-i-dence—"

"Okay, I recall him now. The physicist. Put it on."

OFTEN Nancy Howard had heard the words, "Put it on," without knowing what they meant. She had no idea what was happening behind the closed doors of the private office. Faraway voices sounded, indistinct voices. She caught a flutter of words. "—Now who in the hell—kidnap me?"

Kidnapping! Like an electric shock, the word jolted through her mind. She strained her ears, trying to hear the answer. It came. Something about Preston and Howe, she couldn't tell what. Her heart climbed up in her throat. Her breath came faster. The receiver crackled in her ear. Words were coming through, but she couldn't tell what they were. In his office, Lorton said nothing. The mechanical voice was still.

She erased one word, then another. Very carefully, she typed them in again, then made a face as if she had made another mistake. Again she picked up the eraser.

"What do you think?" Lorton spoke.

"That At-kin-son will talk," the mechanical voice answered.

"Damn!" Lorton said.

"Yes, sir. What are your or-ders, sir?"

Silence came from the office. Nancy held her breath. Tinny voices rattled far away, she could not tell what they were saying. Lorton was silent.

"Or-ders, sir?" the mechanical voice repeated.

"Watch them. If Atkinson—if Number Nine talks, erase him."

"Very well." In the mechanical answer, she caught a hint of satisfaction, of pleasure, as if somewhere, some thing relished this order. "In the pres-ence of the F S B man, sir?"

"Yes, if that is necessary to keep him from talking."

"But the F S B man will see what hap-pens."

"Let him. A whole helluva lot of good it will do him."

"Very well, sir."

Silence again. Nancy tried to type. The errors were real now. Her fingers hit the wrong keys; her thumb found the space bar at the wrong time. She started the final letter all over again, made too many honest mistakes, and had to retype it. Vaguely there sounded in her earphone, faint popping sounds, something like the noise of a pistol exploding far away. There was one thin wail that she thought was someone screaming, then silence again.

"It is finish-ed, sir," the mechanical voice said.

"Good. Carry on," Lorton answered. A soft click sounded in her earphones. She knew what the click meant, that she would hear nothing more at this time. She bent furiously to her typing.

In her mind was no understanding of what she had heard. But one point was clear. At last she had a name. William B. Atkinson. If she could find him, she could find a man who might be able to help her.

A whisper of sound came from behind her. She turned. Giles Lorton stood in the door of his private office.

He was a short man, of a stocky build, with a round impassive face. His eyes were deep-set and they looked furtively out at the world from behind bushy eyebrows. Every time she saw him, she had the impression of some beast of the jungle peering out through a fringe of thorny foliage at the world beyond the edge of the green tangle that was its home.

Lorton was well dressed. The best tailors made his suits, his shirts were hand-made, his ties hand-painted. A diamond ring glittered on his right hand, on his left wrist was a thick-cased diamond studded wristwatch. The best of everything, this he had. Power, and the knowledge of it, flowed out from him like a tangible electric force.

A little cry sounded in her throat at the sight of him.

He stood there in the doorway somberly regarding her.

CHAPTER THREE

LIKE A mounting, mushrooming atomic explosion, fear rose in his brain. The impulse in him was to run. He fought it. His gaze went around the laboratory. If a ball of swirling blackness was forming there, he could not see it. Lights bright enough for taking motion pictures spat at him like angry cats. Atkinson had had the impression that there was safety in light. It had been a mistaken impression. He had even tried to use a light weapon. Though the weapon had failed, January remembered that the ball of darkness had tried to twist away from it. This was a fact worth remembering. The light weapon had not stopped the *penth* but the creature had slowed when confronted with that intense beam of brilliant illumination.

There was nothing in the lab that he could see.

The setting in the ring had ceased to glow.

Had something, partially evoked when he picked up the telephone, gone back into nothingness when he replaced the headset on its cradle? He did not know. *Was his mind being read?* Had his intention to call FSB headquarters and report what had happened here been deduced from the fact that he had picked up the telephone or had something slipped inside his mind and read the intention there?

He did not know which it was or that either solution was true. He did not know—anything.

There was one way he could find out. If you dialed GARfield 0001-2 you got the time. Surely no one could object to him knowing the correct time. He reached for the phone.

The glow appeared in the ring.

Hastily he took his hand away from the phone.

The glow died in the stone.

Then his mind wasn't being read. His intentions were being deduced from his actions. He felt a little better at the thought that his hidden mental world was safe. He could think in safety. But not much better as he realized that even if his mind wasn't being read he was being watched.

Something here in this lab was watching him. Something saw him pick up the telephone. Something got ready to act each time he tried to talk. Something didn't want him to make a report.

At the other end of this telephone, at the other end of any telephone, was help. When his report went through, top-flight minds would be called into consultation. The entire resources of the FSB would be at his disposal. Agents would fly into Chicago, they would come in by train and bus. Very quietly the local and state police would be notified, their assistance asked and received. A cordon could be thrown around and through the city until no alley cat could pounce on a rat without the action being noted.

All this if he could use the phone.

The catch was—he couldn't use it.

He had no wish to join Atkinson. If he tried to use the phone, he did not in the least doubt that he would find himself joining that vanished scientist.

What to do?

Carefully he picked up the ring from the desktop. He picked up his briefcase. From the floor under the desk where it had fallen he scooped up the tiny weapon that Atkinson had used, slipped it in his pocket.

He went quietly out the door.

THE SECOND the door closed behind him, he began to run. No fleet-footed halfback sprinting through a broken field, with a touchdown, a Bowl game, and a professional contract waiting for him when he crossed the goal line, ever did a better job of zigging and zagging, of ducking and dodging, than did Joe January on this occasion. He didn't know he was being followed, he didn't know he wasn't, he just knew there was a chance that he was being pursued. He didn't know whether he could outrun his pursuer or whether he couldn't, he just knew he had to try. He ducked down an alley; he cut across a vacant lot at imminent risk of his life and ducked across a street humming with traffic. Parked at the curb, he saw a vacant cab. He jumped into the backseat. "Downtown, as fast as you can make it."

The driver grinned at him. "Whatsamatter, did her old man come home unexpectedly?"

"I'll say he did. Get this crate in gear and get moving."

He sank back on the cushions of the cab, panting and exhausted, but alive.

Being alive was more than he had really expected.

The driver took the Outer Drive to the Loop. Traffic swirled around the cab, long, sleek cars gleaming with chromium and stainless steel slid past on the river of black asphalt. January slipped Atkinson's ring on his finger. The red stone remained dull and lifeless.

He took a deep breath that was close to pure relief so great in its intensity as to be almost pathological and fumbled in his pockets for his cigarettes.

In the Loop, he had the driver drop him. Crowds thronged through these streets. January joined them. It felt good to bump elbows with people, it felt good to be pushed and shoved, it felt good to look at lighted show windows. There was comfort in a crowd. People everywhere around him. The deep, dark, and desperate fear that crouched shivering in the corner of his mind began to go away. What did it matter if out there in suburban Chicago a private laboratory stood lonely and empty, its bright lights glaring defiance at something that lurked in corners? Down here in this milling throng, he could forget all about that laboratory. It didn't matter to any of these people here. What did it matter to him?

He was kidding himself and he knew it. That lab did matter to him. Although they didn't know it, it mattered to these people here on these streets. Maybe it mattered as much as living or not living. Maybe it mattered as much as the difference between freedom and slavery. Maybe—

A drug store caught his eye. He went in.

"A private phone booth? At the rear, sir," the girl in the cashier's cage told him.

He dialed the long distance number, the phone clicked and hummed, a voice said: "Yes."

He was through to help!

"Wire this."

"Right. Shoot."

"To: Chief, FBS, From: January, Chicago. Priority: Top. Subject: Routine check of William B. Atkinson…"

So far he got. But no farther. There was a slight delay, as if something had lost him momentarily. But only for a moment. Then the stone in the ring began to glow again.

"Waiting for the message," the voice spoke from the other end of the wire.

His eye on the glowing stone, Joe January spoke: "No message." And hung up.

Reluctantly, as if something hated to let go, the glow died in the ring.

Joe January wiped spurting sweat from his face and stepped out of the phone booth.

IN SELECTING its personnel, the Federal Security Bureau had had access to all governmental data on this subject, together with the testing techniques that had been developed since the days of the Alpha test of World War I. In choosing the men to work for it, the Bureau had set up tests that automatically excluded from employment all except exceedingly tough-minded, clear-thinking, hard-boiled skeptics who believed nothing that they heard, nothing that they read, and little that they saw with their own eyes. Even more than these qualities, men were selected for mental balance, poise, the ability to light on their mental feet in most situations and to stay there. Men with minds like the physical balance of a cat, these were what the Bureau wanted.

When he came out of this phone booth, with sweat spurting from him, Joe January needed all the mental balance the Bureau testing technicians thought he had, needed it just to stay sane.

He had been followed, he was being followed now, he could not see or otherwise detect the thing that followed him. If there had been a touch of paranoia anywhere in his mind, this situation would have triggered it into explosive violence. He would have run shrieking from the drug store, he would have dived headlong and screaming into the throngs outside, the police would have gathered him in, strong sedation, possibly a straightjacket would have been needed to force him to be quiet.

Days, possibly weeks later, fingerprints would have revealed his identity; hastily the Bureau would have sent men to investigate him, doctors to treat him. Probably the medicos would have decided they were trying to treat a mind hopelessly insane. The end would have been some institution, some asylum devoted to the care of the mentally sick. Under proper treatment, he might possibly have recovered, given time, but the treatment would have been lengthy and difficult.

This, if he had been anything except what he was, is probably what would have happened. But he was Joe

January. He ran into a booth and almost knocked down a man in a gray suit, getting a glare from a pair of hot brown eyes in return, and stumbled out into the street, scared half to death but with the thought in his mind that possibly the purpose of this whole maneuver *was* to drive him insane. That thought, plus what he was, saved him. If something was trying to drive him nuts…well…let it. In that challenge, like an agile cat being dropped, he twisted himself around as he fell and kept his mental balance.

He didn't laugh. He couldn't. But he did light a cigarette with only one match.

He thought: "The problem is how to communicate what I know to the Bureau and stay alive while I'm doing it."

It was not a little problem.

First, perhaps, was to make an attempt to locate the thing that followed him. He suspected it was a ball of darkness similar to what Atkinson had called a *penth*. It did not seem reasonable to assume that a human could have shadowed him from the laboratory. But something had. Ergo, it was a *penth,* what the hell ever that was.

STANDING ON the sidewalk, with people brushing past him on both sides, he tried to locate it. On both sides of the street, buildings climbed up into the sky. Office buildings, with most of the windows dark, a few lighted ones marking the spot where some unfortunate clerk had to work overtime, or where some department head had cajoled a stenographer into staying late to take a little lap dictation. Overhead in the sky the lights of helicopters moved like little planets in the night.

So far as he could tell, he was unobserved, but as he turned his head from side to side, he got the impression that a thin shadow stayed always just out of the range of his sight. He jerked around quickly, trying to catch sight of it before it could move.

It was faster than he was, it moved quicker than he could.

To hell with it, then. If it was there, it was there. Presumably he could do nothing about it. Obviously it knew that he was aware of it. Or something back of it knew of his awareness. His flight from the lab, the fact that he had stopped using the phone on two occasions, must have revealed his knowledge of its presence.

The next step was to find out what limits it placed on his actions. It did not permit him to use the phone. This much was certain. What else would it stop him from doing?

Down the street a sign said: *GRANT HOTEL.*

He had registered at this hotel earlier in the afternoon, but until this moment he had forgotten this fact. At the sight of the sign, he walked straight to the hotel, entered the lobby, and went directly to a writing desk.

He had hardly got the sheet of paper on the writing desk and the pen in his hand before the ring began to glow.

Letters were out.

A telegram? He doubted it but it was worth trying. There was a telegraph desk in the corner of the lobby. He went over to it, picked up a message blank and a pencil, groaned, dropped the pad of blanks back on the counter.

"Change your mind?" the girl behind the counter asked.

"Yeah. I think I'll write a letter instead. It's cheaper."

"Our special night letter rates are very reasonable, sir."

"Thanks. I guess not." Still he hesitated at the counter. The ring had glowed when he picked up the pencil and the pad, but had gone out when he laid them down. Apparently talk was not verboten. Or did that depend on what he said and to whom he said it? He eyed the girl behind the desk. She had platinum hair and false eyelashes. Her nails were done in scarlet and her blouse puffed out in the places where a blouse ought to puff out.

To his mind, she looked like a girl who didn't intend to spend all her life behind the counter of a telegraph office. Her plans included better things.

"What time you get off, honey?" January said.

"What?" Her eyes flashed over him, appraising him with all the expertness of a girl looking for a man whose bankroll matched her aspirations. "When I get off, I'm busy," she said. Picking up a pad of messages, she began to read them.

JANUARY moved away from the counter. Even if talk was not forbidden, he did not relish the thought of trying to tell this peroxide creature that he was a member of the FSB, that he had seen a ball of blackness gobble up a prominent scientist, that he couldn't report this information to his headquarters without being gobbled up himself, and would she please report it for him?

Why wasn't talking forbidden too? For that matter, why didn't the ring glow all the time? The *penth* was always there, watching him. Why didn't the ring reveal its presence?

He decided that as long as the *penth* just watched him, it remained invisible—and harmless. In this invisible condition the ring did not detect it. Apparently in order to harm him, the *penth* had to become visible. As it started to become visible, the ring detected its presence, probably by means of powerful electromagnetic radiations the *penth* emitted in the process of materialization.

The explanation made sense. For all he knew, it might even be true. What was a *penth*? Atkinson had said that somebody by the name of Michaelson had discovered, invented, created, knew about, or was in some manner responsible for the existence of that blob of darkness. Who was Michaelson?

The name woke lingering echoes in his mind. He had known, or heard of, a man by that name, but at the moment, he couldn't recall who Michaelson was. Some scientist, he thought, but what kind of a scientist or where he lived, January could not recall.

Why was he allowed to talk?

There was only one answer he could see. It was an answer that did not please him at all but one that could be easily checked. Outside the hotel, he looked up and down the street. A blue-coated figure was loafing at the corner. January moved straight toward the cop.

"Officer—" As he spoke, the ring began to glow.

"What is it?" the cop inquired.

"Nothing," he answered. "I had a question, but I just remembered the answer myself." Turning, he walked away. He saw now why he was allowed to talk. He could talk to the girl in the telegraph office, he could probably try to talk to anybody on the street. They wouldn't believe him, probably they would think he was drunk. But the minute he tried to talk to someone in authority, the *penth* was on the job.

Probably the cop on the corner would not understand him either, but the cop would almost automatically arrest him and book him to be held for observation and questioning. There his identity would be revealed, a report would go forward through routine channels to the FSB, and someone would immediately call who would at least try to understand him.

Hence—no talk to cops.

He had information that was of vital importance, but he couldn't communicate it. He was under embargo, under interdict, excommunicated from contact with his fellows.

Which brought him full circle back to his original problem. Somehow he had to duck that *penth,* and get lost.

The question was—how?

In the busy streets of Chicago's Loop a man was shadowed by a shadow.

"A drink is what you need, January," he thought. He

moved toward a saloon. He hardly noticed the man in the gray suit fall into step beside him. In this crowd, anybody going in your direction was likely to seem to be walking beside you.

"Turn right at the next corner," the man in the gray suit spoke.

"What?"

"And keep walking," Gray Suit answered. January recognized him as the man he had bumped into in the drug store.

"Who the hell are you?"

"Keep walking and don't argue," Gray Suit said.

January kept walking. Automatically his lips straightened into a knife-edge line. He measured Gray Suit for heft and build, deciding exactly where he would hit him first and how hard. The fellow didn't look too tough.

The FSB man had already concluded he could take Gray Suit when he realized that the man in the brown suit on his left was also keeping pace with him, walking in step with him in fact. Gray Suit wasn't alone. He had Brown Suit with him.

Glancing over his shoulder, January caught a glimpse of a hard face following right behind him. Blue Suit!

The three men almost surrounding him, they reached the corner.

"Turn right," Gray Suit said, an edge to his voice.

Joe January turned right.

CHAPTER FOUR

LORTON moved quietly across the office and stood looking down at Nancy Howard. A hint of amusement lurked deep in his eyes but his face was somber.

"Working late?"

"Yes. There were some letters that had to be finished. I was going to bring them in for your signature." She felt her voice flutter.

"You seem to work late rather often."

"Oh, I don't mind." Had he gotten suspicious of her? She tried to smile, a failing effort, for in her heart there was fear of this man. "Would—would you like me to take some dictation for you?"

"I—" He really hadn't heard what she had said. His mind was elsewhere. He looked at the letter she was typing, then at the copy she had taken from her typewriter and had laid aside, intending to destroy it later.

"You seem to make a great many mistakes."

"I'm sorry. I guess I'm not very good at typing yet. But I'm trying hard to learn."

"Ah."

He stood looking down at her. His hand moved. Her first startled thought was that he was trying to touch her. She squealed, jumped back. But his hand was not moving toward the area where no padding was necessary. He grabbed the cords of the earphones, jerked the headset from her.

She shrank back in the chair.

Swiftly, efficiently, he inspected the earphones. Her heart climbed all the way up into her mouth. Was the speaker in the left earphone well enough hidden to pass inspection?

He missed it.

She breathed easier.

Then he took the plastic cords in both hands and snapped them. Nancy Howard stopped breathing. The cords were plastic tubes designed to conduct sound. When he broke them the tiny wires running up to the hidden speaker were revealed.

They stood out as two tiny strands of wire as fine as human hair.

"Ah," Lorton said.

His fingers moved instantly to the transcriber, following the wires. If he followed them far enough—and she had no doubt he would—he would inevitably find the hidden radio receiver. That in turn would lead him to—

Slipping out of the chair, Nancy Howard started running toward the door.

HE REACHED out a long arm and caught her, jerked her back. She tried to break free but he held her easily. Paying no more attention to her than if she did not exist, he picked up the transcriber with his other hand, threw it to the floor. It did not break. He kicked it open.

Revealed was the thimble-sized radio hidden there.

"Well," he said. His eyes came to her. For the first time since she had come to work in the office, she had his complete attention. From the tips of her trim shoes to the bottom of her brown hair, his eyes went over her, not missing a thing.

"I don't seem to recall your name. Nancy something, isn't it?"

"Let me go. I haven't done anything wrong." She tried to pull away. He held her easily.

"That's to be decided. Will you come into my office, please?"

"No."

He didn't argue. He just picked her up and carried her, kicking heels and all, over his shoulder. Inside he slammed shut the door and she heard a lock click. Then he carried her over to the over-stuffed leather chair and dropped her.

She began to scream.

He shrugged. "Yell your head off. Nobody will hear you. First—"

His fingers explored her body. If she had hidden a pistol or a knife or even a long pin anywhere in her clothes, his exploration would have revealed it. She tried to resist, discovered that resistance was useless, and quit trying.

"No weapon," he said. "Next—" He forgot her again. She came to her feet, tried to straighten out her disarranged clothes, and headed again for the door. He didn't even look up.

The door was locked. The knob rattled in her hand but would not turn. Lorton paid no attention to her. She moved quickly toward the windows, intending to open them and scream out into the Chicago night.

The windows were sealed permanently, the plastic panes were almost an inch thick.

"Don't try to jump through one of them," Lorton said. "You'll only get a nasty bump."

She moved toward the telephone.

That got his attention. "Sit down," he said.

"But—"

"Or I'll knock you down." He doubled his fist and she collapsed into the leather chair.

His search of the office was as thorough as his search of the earphones had been. Watching him with fear crawling inside her, Nancy realized that he was a man who missed few bets, made few mistakes. The transmitter was hidden under the desk itself, but Lorton found it and knew what it was. He ripped off the tape that held it in place and stood up with it in his hands.

"A transmitter here and a receiver in the outer office," he said. His eyes came down to her. "What have you heard, Nancy?"

"N—nothing. I don't know what you're talking about. What is that thing? Why did you smash my transcriber? You'll get into trouble for this." Fear was an inarticulate panic crawling inside of her. "Let me go. I haven't done anything. I don't know what you're talking about."

"You said that before," he said.

She could see he was having fun, that he was playing a cat-mouse game with her. But he was also a little worried, not too badly worried. No problem could be serious enough to cause him real worry. "Why did you listen to my private conversations?"

"I didn't, I don't know—"

"What have you heard?"

"Nothing. What was there to hear? I—" She broke off under the pressure of his eyes. He was thinking about the fact that she had listened to his private conversations but the look in his eyes told her he was beginning to think more about something else—that she was a woman. The fear in her rose until it began to block her vocal chords. She made gasping sounds deep in her throat.

"Tell me why you did this."

SHE COULDN'T speak, but she shook her head. If she told him why she had done this, she did not know what would happen but she knew her only hope of safety lay in not revealing her secret. Until he knew why she had installed the hidden radio equipment, he would hesitate.

"Who else was in this with you? Who helped you?"

"I'm an FSB agent—" The words came unbidden to her lips. All she knew about the FSB was that the voice had said that an agent of this organization was interviewing somebody by the name of Atkinson. Lorton hadn't liked that. He would like it even less if he thought she was such an agent, perhaps he would hesitate to do anything to her. "I work for the FSB. You better be careful."

For a moment he looked startled and surprised. Then he laughed deep in his throat. "Quit lying."

"It's true. You'll find out that it's true." She saw he didn't believe her but she also saw he was not certain. He took a quick stride across the office, came back to face her. "What is the FSB?"

"It's—" She didn't know. The lack of real knowledge was visible on her face. "You'll find out."

He thought she was lying but he wasn't quite certain. Until he knew, he would take no definite action. Hope stirred in her like the first faint lights of dawn after a hurricane. Again Lorton took that quick step across the room. She saw there was a definite spot worn in the thick rug where he had walked. He shook his head. "We'll see." His hand moved to his wrist.

There was a soft click somewhere. She cried out in fear and tried to shrink deeper into the corner of the leather chair.

With the click there appeared two feet above his desk a swirling ball of blackness. It seemed to come from nowhere and it came instantly, as if in response to a command. It swirled there, not spinning but in motion none the less.

"Yes," a voice spoke.

Nancy Howard sank even deeper into the corner of the chair. This was the voice she had heard in this office. It came from the ball of blackness. Lorton answered.

"I have discovered that a girl who works in my office has been spying on me and has listened to our conversations. She claims she works for the FSB. I think she is lying but I am not absolutely sure. What suggestions can you make?"

"I will look at her," the mechanical voice said. The ball of blackness moved. It hung a foot away from her face. She shrank from it. Within that sphere of blackness, she had the impression something was *looking* out at her. No known organs of vision were involved, no eyes were visible, perhaps looking was not the correct word to describe that inspection, perhaps *awareness* came closer to the actual process, but whether or not the ball looked at her, it was certainly aware of her. She had the impression that it probed every molecule of her body, that before its penetrating awareness, she stood utterly naked and alone. A cry formed in her throat and was choked off.

"I see," the voice said.

"What shall I do?" Lorton questioned.

"I can e-rase her," the voice said. At the words, the ball seemed to move closer to her, as if it was eager for the task at hand. Her lips moved. Somewhere in her soul something was praying. But no words came.

"No," Lorton said. "We have to know about her."

"Very well." Reluctance sounded in the voice. "I will send an ambulance and two men. Bring her here and we will question her."

"No!" She screamed a single word and tried to get to her feet. Lorton forced her back into the chair. The ball vanished.

"What was that? What are you going to do with me?"

"Shut up," Lorton said.

She collapsed in the chair.

THE TWO men were not long in coming. Lorton let them in through the door. They wore the white coats of hospital attendants and they carried a folding stretcher. They looked questioningly at Lorton and he nodded toward Nancy. Mechanically, as if this was a matter of no concern to them, they moved toward her.

The sight of the two men moving toward her aroused in her the knowledge that if she was going to do anything, it had to be now. She leaped to her feet, tried to run. They grabbed her. She tried to fight. In that struggle her clothes were literally torn from her body but she was still trying to fight, down on the floor with one man lying across her, when she felt the hypodermic bite into her hip.

The drug, whatever it was, acted quickly. Five minutes later, completely unconscious, neatly covered by a white blanket, she was on the stretcher and was being carried from the room.

JANUARY expected the three men to force him into a taxicab or a car. Or perhaps they would take him to one of the helicopter landing lots in the Loop. But they didn't put him into a cab, a car, or a copter. They marched him straight to Michigan Boulevard, told him to turn left, and took him through the plastic and aluminum doors of one of the most impressive buildings on the street.

As they went through the lobby two white-coated hospital attendants passed them carrying the still body of a young woman on a stretcher. They went through a side entrance where January caught a glimpse of the attendants shoving the stretcher into a waiting ambulance. As the stretcher passed them, Gray Coat, on January's right, gave a startled gasp. The FSB man could not tell whether it was the sight of the girl or of the attendants that startled Gray Coat but the man had certainly recognized either the patient or the attendants. The single start was all the indication Gray Coat gave, then his face was again immediately composed but the look in his eyes indicated growing pressure somewhere inside.

"This way," Gray Coat said, unlocking a door. Beyond the door, steps led downward.

Below was the basement. Below that was the sub-basement. Here, on the sub-basement level, heat and water were brought into the building. Here also were the wires for light and telephone. Here, also, a connection was made to the extensive miniature railroad system that lies under Chicago—and under every other large city, a sub-surface railroad that brings coal, freight, and many other supplies to the large buildings, and in turn takes away everything from some finished products of the manufacturers to waste paper and rags.

Blue Suit pushed a button.

"Okay, boys, get going," Gray Suit said. "I'll take it from here."

Blue Suit and Brown Suit went back up the stairs. January thought of the gun under his left shoulder. They hadn't searched him. He waited until Blue Suit and Brown Suit had had enough time to be out of the building, then pulled the gun.

Gray Suit looked at it. Neither surprise nor fear registered on his lean face. He held out his hand. "Give it to me," he said.

"Go to hell."

Gray Suit shrugged. "Anybody who has enough intelligence to stay sane in your position has too much intelligence to try to use a gun on me."

"Oh," January said. Out of the corner of his eyes he saw that the ring was glowing again. He jerked his head around. In the air behind him a shadow moved. Hastily he handed the gun to Gray Suit. "I didn't know for sure that you and it—" a twist of his head indicated what he meant by it "—were on the same side."

"You know it now." Gray Suit put the gun in his pocket. He looked meditatively at January, seemed about to speak, then changed his mind. Somewhere a bell clanged. A door opened and a miniature electric locomotive appeared pulling a single car. A driver in greasy overalls with his cap pulled down over one eye looked at Gray Suit.

"A couple of passengers, Jim," Gray Suit said. The motorman seemed accustomed to picking up passengers. He nodded. "After you, please," Gray Suit said to January. The single car was half full of trash. The two men sat side by side on wooden boxes at the front end. Its electric headlight providing illumination, the train moved into the tunnel. In this closed space the noise of its passage was thrown back at them from the walls. In semi-darkness broken only by the beam of occasional lamps set in the tunnel overhead, January was aware that Gray Suit was leaning close to him. He felt the man's fingers seek his hand.

"Take this," Gray Suit whispered in his ear.

January's fingers closed over a tiny bottle about the size of a perfume container.

"As soon as we hit a dark place, drink the contents," Gray Suit whispered. His mouth was within an inch of January's ear.

"What?"

"Don't ask questions. Do as you are told now or you will do as you are told the rest of your life." The man's voice was a fierce whisper in January's ear commanding him to obedience. But more than the command, there was a pleading note in it, as if Gray Suit was begging him to obey.

The car shot past a light bulb and vanished into darkness.

"Now." Gray Suit whispered.

JANUARY swallowed the contents of the bottle. It was an oily liquid and it didn't taste good but it produced a prompt and rather pleasant glow in his stomach. Almost immediately the glow seemed to spread outward from his stomach. January had the impression that he could feel his bloodstream pick up the oily liquid and that he could sense it spreading almost inch by inch over his body. Gray Suit, leaning close to him, was whispering again. "When you realized the *penth* would stop you every time you tried to communicate what you knew to anybody who could understand it, you should have gone crazy. Michaelson, and others, did just that. When you didn't, the Brain had no choice except to bring you here, both for examination, to find out how you kept from going crazy, and also for treatment."

"Treatment? Brain? Michaelson?—" January whispered.

They shot under another light and Gray Suit hastily moved away from him. When the light had vanished behind them, the man spoke again.

"You will be questioned. Later you will be strapped to an operating table and treated. After that treatment, you must obey instantly every order given you. Sooner or later, you will have a chance to escape."

"But—"

"The liquid you just drank will neutralize the effect of the treatment. If you hadn't taken it, the treatment you will receive would have robbed you completely of your will to resist. This way, you will retain your faculties. You will have a chance to escape, if you don't give yourself away with some false move."

"Will you be with me?"

"Part of the time I will be. I'll help you if I can, I'll talk to you if I get the chance. But remember that unless you are in some place such as this, where there is so much noise that ordinary talk can't be heard, every word you say can and will be heard. Don't make a false move. Don't speak a careless word."

"Can I think without being overheard?"

"You can think as much as you please. That's all any of us have left, the privilege of thinking. But no matter what we think, we can't do a single solitary damned thing about it. No more questions. From here on, you're on your own."

CHAPTER FIVE

WHEN THE next light shot past overhead, Gray Suit was sitting on the far side of the car from him. Who was this man? What was he doing here? What had he meant by reference to treatment, the Brain, and Michaelson? Was this the same Michaelson that Atkinson had meant? Presumably it was. What was this *penth* that must be following them here through this darkened tunnel? Questions tumbled through January's brain. Gray Suit could certainly answer some of them, but Gray Suit, a somber, hunched figure, squatted on a wooden box on the other side of the car, afraid to talk. The man must have taken a desperate chance even in whispering to him. How much bigger chance had Gray Suit taken in supplying him with the contents of the tiny vial? Only Gray Suit knew.

The train slid to a halt. Gray Suit rose to his feet. With a flashlight, the driver in the engine ahead of them explored the wall beside the cab. So far as January could tell, there were no distinguishing marks on that wall. It was concrete, drippy with moisture, with the marks of the forms in which it had been poured still visible on the surface. The driver seemed to be seeking a particular spot. He grunted, shifted his controls. Gears whined softly and the train moved backward a foot, slowed, stopped. Again the flashlight beam fingered along the wall, found an inch-wide hole, concentrated on that. Somewhere a hidden switch clicked. Air sighed. Ponderously, a section of the concrete wall rolled backward, revealing a lighted passage.

"In there," Gray Suit said.

January stepped from the car. Gray Suit followed. They

entered the passage. With a sound like the hissing of gigantic air brakes, the wall rolled back into place behind them.

The passage hummed with sound. Somewhere ahead of them was activity. They moved forward. The passage opened into a second, bigger, passage. This in turn opened directly into a large room. Here were people and here also was the source of the sound. The room looked like a large laboratory. Around the side of it men and women were busy. Others were coming and going through passages opening out in other directions.

"Who are these people?" January spoke.

"Slaves of Lorton and of his crystal brain," Gray Suit answered. His voice was tight as if his vocal chords were stretched to the breaking point.

"Slaves?"

"The Brain lies beyond," Gray Suit answered. He broke off. Through one of the passages had come two white-coated men carrying a stretcher. On it was the same girl he had seen back in the lobby of the building where they had entered the railway. They had beaten the ambulance here.

"I saw her before," January spoke. Gray Suit did not answer. His eyes were fastened on the stretcher. Muscles tied themselves into knots at the corners of his jaws. On his forehead a vein throbbed visibly. "Your girl?" January whispered.

"Shut up," Gray Suit spoke from the corner of his mouth. Following behind the stretcher was a third man. January took one look at this third man and knew he was seeing somebody important. Not only was importance registered in the expensive clothes, it was shown in his bearing. He was haughty, imperious, lord of all he surveyed. The men and women working at the benches around the room looked sideways at this third man. Not a man spoke, not a man moved, only the sidelong glances showed that they were aware of his presence. The sounds of work went into silence. A man dropped a tool with which he was working. It clattered on the concrete floor. He bent hastily to retrieve it, cringing as his fingers groped for the little wrench he had dropped. His manner was that of a badly frightened man who has made some tiny mistake and is expecting punishment far out of proportion to his error.

"Who's the big shot?" January whispered.

"Lorton," Gray Suit answered mechanically. "It isn't often he comes here."

LORTON spoke sharply to the two men carrying the stretcher. They moved directly across the room and stood waiting in front of a door. Lorton stepped around them. A lighted circle appeared in the center of the door. Lorton stood directly in the light. Some identification process was in operation, January guessed, what it was he did not know.

"Open," Lorton spoke.

The door opened. Beyond it January caught a glimpse of darkness, of shadows moving, of a strange misty half light that was neither light nor shadow but seemed to have existence of its own. The two stretcher-bearers cringed.

"Get in there," Lorton spoke. His voice was that of a man speaking to reluctant dogs, ordering them to obey. Cringing, carrying the stretcher, they passed through. Lorton followed them. The door swung shut.

"That's the room of the Brain," Gray Suit spoke. "They've taken her there." His voice was taut to the breaking point. He moved forward to the door, stood in front of the lighted circle. "Howe," he spoke. "With the F.B.S. agent, as ordered."

There was a moment of silence then a mechanical voice answered. "Take the a-gent to room sev-en."

"Follow me," Gray Suit said.

The room to which January was taken was a prison cell. There was a cot and a bucket in the corner. Nothing else. There was a peephole in the middle of the door. "You'll be sent for," Gray Suit said. "It may be tonight, tomorrow, or next week, but it will be sometime."

Somewhere a thin, distant scream sounded. Gray Suit hastily slammed the door. January sat down heavily on the cot, his hand going into his coat pocket for the inevitable cigarette. His fingers touched there a metallic object, the strange little weapon Atkinson had tried to use against the *penth*. No effort had been made to search him, probably that would come later. So far as he knew, the weapon was useless, but he could not guess what might be made of the fact if it was found in his possession. Likewise the ring. He hid both, wedging them under the mattress on the cot.

The summons for him was not long in coming. The door opened. Peered inside the most wrinkled face he had ever seen. The man who owned the face was diminutive in size, almost a midget. Between the wrinkled face and the diminutive stature the man looked like an over-grown chimpanzee, but his eyes were wiser than the eyes of any monkey. They were almost the wisest, most alert eves the FBS man had ever seen.

"Your turn, bud."

January rose from the cot. The midget led him directly to the door of the room that housed the brain—whatever that was. January took a deep breath. Whatever was in there, he was going to see it. The door opened. He stepped through.

His first dazed impression was that shadows moved away to permit his passage. This room was cold, bitterly cold. He could not guess the temperature but it must have been well below zero. It was a penetrating coldness that went through him, cutting him to the bone. It was an unnatural kind of coldness; a clamminess went with it. Somehow, as he entered this room, he thought of the cold of outer space.

IN THE center of the room rising four feet high from the floor beneath, was a rounded dome of crystal. What the dome was made of January could not distinguish, the thought that came into his mind was that it was made of some kind of plastic. It was almost transparent. Inside it was a tremendously complicated crystal formation. Snowflakes are ice crystals. No two ice crystals are alike. If a million snowflakes had been combined into a single pattern, with every flake uncrushed, with every flake remaining just as it was formed, the resulting formation might have approached the texture of this crystal. Literally hundreds of hair-sized threads led downward from the crystals where they were grouped together into wrist-thick cables that vanished into the floor. The whole surrounding room was one vast switchboard. Whole rows of tiny lights flashed on and off. Behind the shielding of the panels relays clicked, a continuous soft chatter of sound.

Without needing to be told, January knew that this was— the Brain. That it was also the nerve center, the heart and soul, of some vast organization, he could easily guess.

The room that housed the Brain was alive—with shadows. *Penths!* They moved in restless search in every direction. Directly on top of the brain itself, they crouched, a solid, opaque mass. From this mass they were constantly being detached and as constantly returning. At the sight of them, January felt the cold of outer space itself creep into his brain. His flesh crawled.

Standing beside the Brain was—a man. Lorton. The darting *penth* shadows kept completely away from him. They seemed to recognize in him their master and to stay clear. Lorton stood there. His face was impassive. His dark eyes inspected January, missing nothing. He spoke.

"You are an agent of the Federal Bureau of Security?"

"Yes."

"You interviewed a scientist named Atkinson?"

"I did."

"And he attempted to reveal to you certain forbidden information?"

"I do not know whether or not it was forbidden but he attempted to tell me certain things—yes."

"What things?"

"He said he knew what had happened to Preston and Howe."

"You were interested in that?"

"Naturally."

"Atkinson tried to reveal this information to you?"

"He did."

"Did he succeed?"

"He did not."

"Why didn't he?"

January made a gesture with his thumb. "One of those things got him," he answered.

"Ah." The somber eyes were introspective. January had the impression that Lorton was questioning him and listening to his answers and that the Brain was also listening—and checking those answers against information of its own. He did not know what would happen if he tried to lie, but he knew he had no intention of finding out. All around the room relays were clicking softly, lights were flashing, and *penths* were moving in and out of the parent darkness on top of the crystal structure. When they came out they seemed to slide away into nothingness, to vanish, disappear. He could not tell how they disappeared or where they went but his eyes hurt when he tried to follow them as if his eyeballs were wrenched in their sockets. Also he had the impression that he was not receiving the undivided attention either of Lorton or of the Brain, especially of the latter. While the Brain seemed to watch him and listen to him, it also seemed to be watching a dozen other people at the same time, perhaps listening to hundreds. Information seemed to be coming into it, orders going out, as if it was big enough and complete enough to carryon hundreds of different activities at the same time!

UNDER OTHER circumstances, he would have been tremendously awed at this fact. Now it was only one other development in a world turned topsy-turvy.

The mechanical voice spoke. "How did you keep sane when you discovered you were being followed?"

"I almost did go nuts at first."

"But what saved you?"

"I decided the purpose of the whole maneuver was to drive me insane. This, plus the fact that I am sort of tough-minded, saved me, I guess." The last was added doubtfully.

"You are not certain you are sane?" the mechanical voice questioned.

"Not a bit of it," January answered.

The brain was silent. Lorton spoke: "Do you know a woman by the name of Nancy Howard, or Nancy Howe?"

"Howard? Howe. There was a scientist named Howe."

"His sister," Lorton answered. "Somehow he managed to communicate with her shortly after she was taken, with the result that she attempted to spy on me. You may have seen the woman on the stretcher. Do you know her or did you ever see her before?"

"No, to both questions."

"Was she working for the FBS?"

"Not to my knowledge."

"Have you com-muni-cated with the FBS since you last saw At-kin-son?" the mechanical voice spoke from the Brain.

"You know the answer to that better than I do," January answered.

"Yes," the Brain said. There was a moment of silence, then the Brain spoke to Lorton. "Have you reached a dec-i-sion yet?"

"Yes," Lorton said. "Treat him. It may be that I will want to send him back on his job, to report on the activities of the Bureau."

January was silent. Gray Suit had warned him that he would be treated but Gray Suit had not warned him that he might be sent back on his job, to spy for Lorton and the Brain. He tried not to show it but if once he got out of this place and got the chance, no power on earth would keep him from reporting, not to Lorton, but to the FBS.

As if he was reading his mind, Lorton spoke: "I guess you *will* do it, if I want you to." He spoke with a sureness that was full of meaning and the trace of a smile flickered over his dark face. "You can go now."

Although no signal that he had seen was given, when he turned the door was already opening. The wrinkled face of the chimpanzee was peering in at him. The chimpanzee beckoned. In response to the summons, January moved out of this room where relays clicked, lights flashed, where there squatted like a monstrous toad a crystal structure that was actually a brain, where shadows came from nothingness and returned to it, and where the biting cold of outer space chilled with the touch of a nameless horror. Why was that room so cold? Did the Brain require refrigeration? There was no answer, now, possibly there was no answer ever.

The door clicked shut behind him.

They were again in the big room where the men and women worked so busily.

"Call me Mike," the chimpanzee man said.

"Hello, Mike," January answered.

"Hello, yourself. You're a cool customer. Most guys have to be carried when they come out of that place. But you come out walking, and not even shivering." Mike shook his head. A trace of admiration showed in the wise eyes. "But don't try it, pal. Don't try it is all I got to say."

"Don't try what?"

"Don't try to slug me and fight your way out of here. You look like you're thinking about it. It's been tried before and it hasn't worked yet."

"No? There's always a first time."

"A first time, yes, but in this place there's not any second time. Don't try it, pal. Take what ever comes and like it. It's the only way to stay alive." A shudder passed over the slender body.

"Thanks for the indoctrination," January said. "You can call me Joe."

"Sure, Joe. Come with me, Joe."

They moved to another closed door. "Another customer ahead of you. Gotta take turns."

"What happens to me here?"

"This is where you get treated," Mike answered. "But don't worry about it, pal. It won't hurt very much. But you'll never be the same afterward."

"What if I don't want to be treated?"

"Who the hell cares what you want, Joe? It's what you get that makes you fat. Ah, they're finished. You're next."

The door had opened. Out of it came an ordinary hospital rubber-tired table such as is used to move patients to the operating room and back again to their own quarters. Gray Suit was pushing it. On it was the girl. Her face pale and wan; she lay without moving.

January watched her out of sight. It seemed to him that he had been following right behind her forever. She had been just ahead of him in the big building. She had gone into the room of the Brain just ahead of him. Now she was coming out of this place, again just ahead of him. He wondered if be would ever catch up with her.

"Okay. Joe," Mike said. "Just step inside, please, and don't cause any trouble."

Inside the room were two men, who strapped him to the operating table. Somewhere hidden machinery hummed. A light was brought down close to his eyes. It began to whirl. He tried not to watch it. It beat through his eyelids, pouring into his brain.

He lost consciousness without knowing it had happened.

CHAPTER SIX

CONSCIOUSNESS returned slowly to Joe January, bringing with it memories of great pain and the sensation of being pushed and pulled about inside. He had the dazed feeling that something had been done to every molecule in his body, that some pressure had been applied right down to the individual cells and to the submicroscopic structure within them and that each cell and each individual molecule was protesting against this outrage. What had been done to him? He lay still and tried to think about that—and tried not to think. Dazed memories floated through his mind. He waited, patiently, for his mind to clear.

He was in bed in some quiet, dark place. Somewhere in the distance there were confused sounds, he tried to make out what they were, gave up the effort. It was better just to lie still and wait. Something would probably happen. He stirred.

Something did happen. The instant he stirred, there was the sound of soft movement somewhere near him. He caught the faint whisper of footsteps. "No shoes," he thought. Somebody with naked feet was approaching him and taking plenty of care about it. He lay still. A vague shadow moved. A voice whispered: "Mr. January."

It was a woman's voice. He wondered if it was the girl who had been just ahead of him for so long. Had he finally caught up with her? He tried to speak. A grunting sound came from his throat. His vocal chords were not yet ready to function.

"Shhh…" the girl whispered. "You mustn't make that much noise. If you understand me, nod." A hand found his face. He nodded.

Her lips were very close to his ear. "I've got to talk to you."

He nodded.

In the darkness, he could sense her hesitation and her fear. She had something to tell him but she was desperately afraid she would be overheard. He felt her fingers move the sheet covering him and he realized what she was going to do.

"Hey…" he whispered.

"I can't help it, I've got to talk to you."

A split second later she was under the sheet and he was realizing that her feet were not the only part of her that was naked.

The shock completely cleared his mind. "But, damn it—"

"Please."

He could feel her trembling. "Please. There isn't any other way for us to talk. We just don't dare take the chance of being overheard."

"All right," he answered. "But it's a hell of a strain to put on a man."

Her lips less than an inch from his ear, she began to whisper. "I am Nancy Howe. I am the sister of William Henry Howe—"

"What? But he was kidnapped!"

"Not so loud. He was kidnapped and brought here and made into one of Lorton's slaves. He's here now. He brought you here."

GRAY SUIT! This time January managed to keep from starting. He remembered how interested Gray Suit had been in this girl and now he knew why. She was his sister and Gray Suit was one of the missing scientists whose disappearance had prompted the formation of the Federal Security Bureau. Lorton had even asked him if he knew this girl or if she worked for the FSB. Apparently she had been spying in Lorton's office. In swift, terse whispers she told him what had happened. "Before he was kidnapped, William Henry suspected what was happening. He told me his suspicions and said that he thought somebody by the name of Lorton was back of the whole thing. Lorton caught me spying on him and brought me here."

"But why didn't your brother report the whole thing to the authorities?"

"Because he couldn't. He didn't have a chance."

"The hell he didn't. When he grabbed me, he was right in the middle of the Loop."

"That didn't make any difference. He had been treated—he was under the control of the Brain. He couldn't say a word, he couldn't take an action without the Brain's knowledge."

"What?"

"I don't understand the process and he didn't have time to explain it to me but the treatment is given to all the slaves of the Brain. It is part hypnosis, part something else. After they have been treated, the slaves have to obey every order given them. Moreover the Brain is aware somehow of their obedience or lack of it. If they disobey, a *penth* is sent instantly, to warn them. If they disregard that warning, they are destroyed. William Henry could not have gone to the authorities without being killed."

January, with his own grim memories of how the *penth* had followed him, did not in the least doubt that ways existed for removing disobedient slaves. "But he talked to me."

"He took a chance that he wouldn't be overheard."

"Has he been treated?"

"Yes. Naturally."

"But you said that no one could disobey when he had been treated. In talking to me, he disobeyed."

"Yes. The slaves are free to think. Rebellious thinking

can't be detected, but rebellious actions can. He and some others working with him have succeeded in developing an antidote to the treatment process. If taken after the treatment, it is about ten to fifteen per cent effective. If taken before treatment, it is one hundred per cent effective."

"Was that what he gave me in that tiny bottle?"

"Yes. He gave me the same antidote before I was treated. You and I are the only two free people in this place. And the Brain doesn't know it."

She sounded as if she thought that meant something. January tried to see what it meant. He couldn't see where it meant anything. "But even if we can act against the Brain, we won't get anywhere. A *penth* will catch us—"

"That's just it," she answered. "The treatment process is what enables the Brain to know where we are at all times. If we can get out of here, untreated, the Brain can't send *penths* after us *because it won't know where to find us.* So far as it can tell, we will simply have disappeared. We will have a chance to report this whole thing to the proper authorities."

"Hell on wheels, what's holding us? Let's get going!"

SHE CAUGHT him before he could move, pulled him back. "My brother says that as soon as we have made our report to the authorities, we are to find some way to communicate with a man by the name of Atkinson, that this Atkinson has developed a weapon which will repel the *penths.* It's a light weapon, of some kind. My brother says that any competent technician can duplicate it. Armed with this weapon, we are to come back to this place and destroy the Brain. He says that without the *penths*, the Brain is helpless."

"Atkinson!" January had heard only this one word. "We are to go to Atkinson?"

"Yes. Do you know him?"

"Yes. He's dead."

"Oh." Her whisper was a strangled sound in the darkness. "My brother didn't know. He has been relying on Atkinson. What happened?"

"A *penth* got him. And not only that but I have his weapon."

"You do?" Hope stirred again in the whispered voice.

"Yeah. It doesn't work."

In the darkness, he could feel her shudder. "But my brother will have to remain here, under the control of the Brain. To save him, we will have to come back. To come back, we simply have to have a weapon that will stop the *penths*."

"I saw Atkinson use the weapon on a *penth*. It slowed the beast but did not stop it."

"Well—"

"Shhh!" Soft footsteps sounded in the darkness. He caught Nancy's shoulder, discovered that he didn't have her shoulder, and hastily moved his hand. The footsteps came nearer. A hand touched the bed. January sat up, his fist cocked. "Are you conscious?" a voice whispered.

The speaker was Henry William Howe, alias Gray Suit. January and the girl spoke together.

"I've brought your clothes," Howe said. "You've got to get out of here, right now. The Brain is busy doing something, what I don't know. But you two have got to be gone while it is fully occupied."

In the darkness they dressed hastily. In a terse whisper, January explained about the ring and the weapon that Atkinson had once owned. "I'll get them," Howe said. He moved away into the darkness.

When he returned, he carried the two objects. January slipped the ring on his finger. With that warning device in operation, he felt a lot safer. "Here's something else," Howe said. January's fingers closed around his gun.

"If a slave of the Brain tries to stop you, use it," Howe whispered. "Don't hesitate. He'll thank you. There isn't a person here who wouldn't die gladly if dying gave somebody a chance to stop Lorton and his brain."

He led them through the darkness. They did not go back through the main caverns. Howe used a tiny flashlight and he moved fast, as if something had to be done quickly. The flashlight revealed a wooden door, which he opened. Beyond lay more darkness with a far-off roar.

"This is the same way you came in," Howe whispered. "I don't dare take the risk of leading you directly to the surface overhead. No matter how busy the Brain is, it wouldn't miss that. You will have to find your own way out of here. If a train catches you, press back against the wall. There's clearance almost everywhere. Good luck." He pressed the flashlight into January's hands.

"Why don't you come with us?" January questioned.

"I don't dare," Howe answered. "No matter where I went, the Brain could locate me. There is some sort of a radio detection device connected with the treatment process, some way by which the Brain can locate instantly any person who has been treated. If I go with you, it will find me, and you too. I've got to stay here. Get going, you two. And— good luck."

THEY STEPPED down to the track. The wooden door closed shut behind them. Staying carefully away from the third rail that powered the electric locomotives that ran on these tracks, they moved furtively through the darkness.

January watched the ring on his finger. The stone did not glow. If they were followed, the *penth* was remaining intangible. "Do you have any idea how to get out of here?" the FSB agent asked.

"Not the slightest," the girl answered. "But there's a way

out somewhere."

They moved forward in the darkness. Overhead occasionally they heard deep roaring sounds, trains passing on the surface. January's watch said three o'clock. He assumed it was three o'clock in the morning, but the watch had stopped. Behind them came a rumble. The rails throbbed.

"Train coming," Nancy Howe whispered.

As they moved to the wall, the headlight caught them. Brakes screeched. January slipped the gun from his pocket. If the driver was Jim, the engineer who had brought him here—

Sparks showed from the third rail as the miniature electric locomotive slid to a halt. An astonished voice said: "Now what in hell could you two be doing down in this place? In the park, yes. On the beach, yes. But here, no!"

January turned the beam of the flashlight into the cab. The round face of an elderly Irishman looked back at him. He hastily slipped the gun back into his pocket.

"We were on a treasure hunt," he said. "The clues led us into the basement of a Loop building."

"Treasure hunt, is it? All I can say is that it's mighty lucky for you the fool killer has got so much business elsewhere. Otherwise he'd have the two of you for sure. Get in that car."

The car was full of ashes. Like two bedraggled rats trying to escape from an alley, Joe January and Nancy Howe squatted on top of the ashes. The little train rattled through the darkness, slid to a halt again, this time in front of an open doorway.

"Get out of here," the engineer told them. "And be careful to keep your eye out for that fool killer. He'll get you sure."

They stepped into a sub-basement, went upward past the

eyes of a startled janitor who plainly thought they had been smooching somewhere down below. They emerged from the building in the heart of the Loop, with the bright sun of high noon shining in the sky overhead and hungry pedestrians hurrying along the street to wherever pedestrians are always hurrying to.

Traffic whistles shrilled, cars, trucks, streetcars, and busses rolled along the street. In the sky, helicopters beat lazy wings. Far overhead silver wings glistened, the noon flight for Paris. January sucked the sights and the sounds into his mind. Here were thousands of people going about their normal business. None of them had ever heard of such a thing as a crystal brain, or a *penth*. None of them even guessed that such things existed.

The girl clung to him. For the first time he got a good look at her. He liked what he saw. "You haven't screamed once," he said.

"I did my screaming earlier," she answered. "I hope I don't have to do any more of it."

"You and me both," he answered fervidly. His eyes took in the hurrying throngs on the street. "And all this fool killer bait too, although they don't know it."

"What do we do first?" Nancy Howe questioned.

"I'm going to the nearest telephone and put in a call," he said. "You're going to stay back out of sight and watch me while I'm on the phone. If I hang up without completing the call, you're going to get lost—fast."

"Why?"

He told her why. Her face was already pale and cut by lines of fatigue. As he spoke, the lines deepened.

In the phone booth, he picked up the receiver, dialed a number. The stone in the ring remained dull and lifeless but it seemed to him that somewhere in some far distance he could hear relays clicking. He shook the illusion out of his mind.

The long distance connection was made; he spoke into the phone. Then, as the stone in the ring began to glow, he hung the phone back on the hook.

Either Howe had made a mistake in estimating the efficiency of the antidote to the treatment he had undergone or the elderly Irishman in the locomotive of the miniature railway had been a slave of the Brain.

It didn't much matter who had made the mistake.

All that mattered was that the mistake had been made.

Again he was being followed by a *penth*.

As he stepped out of the phone booth, every muscle in his body was trembling and sweat was spurting from every pore.

In the front of the drug store, a frightened girl slid hastily out of the door and disappeared into the noonday crowds.

CHAPTER SEVEN

WHEN JANUARY came out of the drug store, he headed straight for the nearest saloon. Fortunately the place turned out to be exactly that, a high ceiling room with a long mahogany bar, oak tables, and brass spittoons, operating in utter defiance of the polished chromium and glass table places which catered to the more modern crowds. The bartender took one look at the FSB agent and promptly set the bottle on the bar. He took two drinks straight and they helped. There was a steam table at the end of the bar. He took the bottle with him while he inspected the sandwiches— thick slices of ham and fragrant cheese on rye bread. It seemed days had passed since he had eaten last. The food helped too, maybe more than the whiskey, but he Clung to the bottle, taking a drink after each sandwich. It was no way to eat and drink, so he stopped eating.

He wondered about the girl, had she escaped? He hoped there was only one *penth* and that it had followed him. He assumed it had. There was a way to check that, of course. He went into the phone booth and checked, coming quickly out again with the knowledge that it *had* followed him. He took two more drinks. Of course there might have been two *penths*. One might have followed him and the other might have followed Nancy.

At the thought, he took two more drinks.

Why was he still alive?

The only reason he could see was that the Brain hated to use its *penths* where they could be seen in operation. A man in a crowd vanishing the way he had seen Atkinson vanish would create quite a stir, attracting far too much attention. Apparently the Brain did not want to arouse curiosity, yet, apparently it wanted to keep its existence hidden, but January did not doubt that the time would come when the Brain would announce its presence.

The potentialities of the thing were beyond imagination. With it, Lorton could rule a world. Slaves of the Brain installed in the right places, the police force, the governmental agencies, would give Lorton more power than Caesar, Hitler, or Stalin ever had. What could be done to stop it? What could be done to get rid of that invisible *penth* that followed January, watching every move?

Sometime in the middle of the afternoon the answer occurred to January. It was so simple he wondered why he had not thought of it before. Paying his bill, he left the saloon.

The girl at the reception desk was a very superior creature. Her nails were perfect, her hair-do was just right, and her manner was nicely calculated to throw a chill into anybody who accidentally wandered into these exalted premises. Her motto was "No peddlers allowed." Privately it was her thought that if any peddling was going to be done around these premises, she was going to do it. She looked up as this unshaven, unkempt man approached her desk.

From his appearance, she judged he had slept in his clothes. From his breath, she was quite certain he was drunk. She couldn't understand quite how he had got up here, obviously he hadn't used the private elevator, but she assumed he had used one of the regular elevators, then walked up the stairs to this level. It didn't much matter how he had gotten here, he could go back the same way. She froze her face as he approached her desk.

"Is Mr. Lorton in, honey?"

For a moment, so outraged was she at being called honey by so disreputable a person, she considered telling him bluntly that Mr. Lorton was not in. But that would be too easy. She would needle him first. "Do you have an appointment?" she asked sweetly.

"No, can't say I do. Is he in?"

"Yes, he's in. Whom shall I say is calling?"

The bum grinned at her without malice. Reaching inside the waist-high door, he clicked the inside latch, and walked in. And walked right past her. "Don't say anybody is calling, honey."

JOE JANUARY was not awed by superior creatures nor was he impressed by them. To his mind, they came a dime a dozen. He walked past her and through the big door.

Lorton looked up from his desk. January closed the door behind him. He had never seen a man with more surprise on his face than was on Lorton's face now. Perhaps his presence here accounted for it, perhaps it was the gun he held drawn as he came through the door. He moved swiftly forward until he was standing just across the desk from Lorton.

"At this distance, I can't miss," he said. "The slugs in this gun go right through you. If you as much as bat an eyelash without my permission, I'll put all six of them through you. Get your hands up."

Lorton lifted his hands. "How—how did you get here? You—you were—"

"Treated?" January supplied the word. "Maybe it didn't take."

Lorton's face registered consternation, "But— that isn't possible. It always takes. It—" He made a motion to bring his hands down.

January's finger tightened on the trigger of the gun. "If you are thinking a *penth* can take me, think again. I'll put six bullets through you before the *penth* is finished with me. You made a mistake."

The hands went swiftly up again. Lorton's lips moved.

"And after the bullets go through me, then what?" he said.

January sighed. "I knew you would think of that." He shrugged. "Sometimes a man has got to die, Lorton. After I put the bullets through you, I might die. It depends on whether or not the Brain is capable of carrying on without orders from you. I don't know the answer to that but I got to take a chance. There are some things I want to know. First, I got a little follower."

"You mean a *penth?*"

"Yes. How'd I get it?"

"I—I don't know."

"You don't know?" Was the man lying?

"I—I can find out."

"How?"

"I'll make contact with the Brain." January was silent, considering the problem. Any way he turned, he was taking a chance. "All right. Make contact. But remember how fast I can pull the trigger on this." He wiggled the gun.

"I'll have to send out the signal."

"All right. Send it out. But don't make any mistakes."

Lorton's right hand moved to the watch on his left wrist. He pressed something there, what it was January could not see. The response he could see. A *penth* buzzed in the room. January almost pulled the trigger then. It took every erg of will power he possessed to keep from emptying the gun. Lorton spoke not to him but to the *penth,* "That FSB agent is here."

"I know," the mechanical voice answered. "I—I could not an-tic-i-pate his intention. I—I—"

If this was the Brain speaking, and January was sure it was, then the Brain was worried.

"He says he is followed by a *penth.*"

"He is telling the truth."

"Damn you!" For an instant, violent rage sounded in

Lorton's voice. "Then you knew he was coming here. Why didn't you tell me?"

"I couldn't. I decided it was best—"

"Why didn't you destroy him?"

"I—" The Brain seemed to be having trouble finding answers. Under other circumstances, January might have found a sort of grim satisfaction in this spectacle of Lorton arguing with the Brain but the ice he was skating on was far too thin for him to enjoy anything.

"I—I can destroy him now," the Brain volunteered. On January's finger the already glowing ring became a more violent red. He knew the *penth* that had followed him was being materialized in the room.

"No!" Lorton screamed the command. "He'll kill me first."

"How right you are," January said. The muzzle of the gun did not waver from Lorton's chest. "Six bullets. All of them going right through you."

THERE WAS consternation on Lorton's face. Somewhere else there was consternation too. Again January had the impression of far-off relays clicking violently as the crystal brain sought to find a solution to this problem. "I-but-it will be fast," the Brain said.

"But not fast enough," Lorton shouted.

"Right again," January said.

"But if he kills you, I will kill him," the Brain said.

"What good will that do me?" Lorton said grimly.

"You never miss a point," January said. "The only mistake you ever made lay in not realizing that if you threatened a man too much—and the little pal who has been going around with me qualifies as too much of a threat—there comes a time when a man gives himself up as being as good as dead already. When a man reaches that point, he is really dangerous." He hesitated for a moment, then spoke grimly. "I passed that point some time back."

"But what shall I do?" the Brain spoke from the *penth*.

"How did I get my little pal?" January spoke. "That puzzles me."

"Shall I tell him?" the Brain spoke to Lorton.

"Of course. He'll kill me. He means it."

"The engineer who picked you up on the railway is my man," the Brain answered. "He reported your presence. I tried to call you back. At this point, I realized that somehow my treatment process had failed. I am trying now to discover—" The scratchy mechanical voice went into silence.

"The Irishman," January said. "And he seemed such a nice guy." He meditated darkly on the iniquity of people who seemed to be nice guys.

"Can I take my hands down?" Lorton spoke.

"Nope. Keep 'em up."

"But I just want to open my desk drawer."

"Something interesting in there?"

"Very. Take a look and see." Lorton licked his lips.

Cautiously, January moved around the desk. He stepped behind Lorton. "You open the drawer, sweetheart." The muzzle of the gun was pushed against Lorton's backbone. "Don't make any mistakes."

Very gently, Lorton slid open the drawer. January looked down at what was revealed. Each held by a rubber band, there were stacks of bills there. The one on top was a thousand-dollar bill. January took a deep breath.

"They're all thousands," Lorton spoke. "Twenty-five in each package."

January laughed. "No, thanks, sweetheart."

Lorton spoke: "What do you want? You can have it. Women—"

"One would suit me," January answered. "I want

something else."

"What?" Lorton sounded as if he was about to take hope again.

"Three things. First, call off the *penth* that is following me."

"Granted. Remove it." The last two words were spoken to the ball of darkness hovering in the air.

"But—" the Brain protested.

"Do as you are told!" Lorton shouted.

"Very well."

THERE WERE two balls of darkness in the room, the one that obeyed Lorton and through which he spoke to the Brain, the second that followed January. The second one was incompletely materialized at present. As the Brain spoke, it swirled, vanished. Had it gone back to the Brain? January, remembering the way the *penths* had appeared and disappeared in that ice cold room that housed the brain, suspected it had, suspected also that the journey had not been made through any kind of space the human mind knew. But that was something else. He had no time for such speculations.

"It's done," Lorton said.

"The second thing, if there is a *penth* following Nancy Howe, I want it called off."

"Is there?" Lorton spoke.

"No," the Brain answered. Agitation sounded in the mechanical voice. "They tricked me. I—I thought one was enough. They separated suddenly. Before I could send the second *penth*—"

"Good," January said. And meant it. The wave of relief that swept through him was a heady dizziness in his mind. She was safe. She had gotten away!

"What's the third thing?" Lorton questioned.

"How do you call your little pal?" He nodded toward the *penth* remaining in the room. "That is, how do you get him to come when you want him?"

Lorton exhibited his watch. "A special radio transmitter is built into the case of this watch. When I send out a signal the Brain sends a *penth* to me."

"Good," January said. "Good. Send him away."

For a split second Lorton hesitated. January had the impression that the Brain, which must be watching and hearing everything happening here, was also hesitating, and trying to decide what action he would take next. He pushed the muzzle of the gun against a vertebra in Lorton's backbone.

"That's all," Lorton said. "Take it away."

The *penth* swirled and vanished.

"I feel almost naked without one of those things breathing down my neck," January said. He eyed the crystal setting of the ring. The glow was gone. No materialized or partly materialized *penth* was present in the room. The Brain was cut off from all knowledge of what was happening here. "Take off your watch," he said.

"Huh? What? I mean—"

"Take it off," January said. No muleskinner ever got more snap in the crack of a whip than January did in his voice. Reluctantly Lorton slid the watch from his hand. January took it from his hand, examined it carefully. "How do you use it to call one of your little pals?" he said.

"Just press the stem," Lorton answered.

The FSB man carefully placed the watch in his coat pocket. He moved around to the far side of the desk. Lorton watched him. "I assume you wanted to talk to me without the Brain knowing what you were saying?"

"You're partly right, sweetheart. I want to talk. You're right that far. But not to you." He pointed to the phones.

"Which one of these is a direct wire to central?"

LORTON DIDN'T answer but his straying eyes revealed which phone it was. January picked it up. He laid the receiver on the desk. "I'm going to dial a number and I'm going to do a little talking. If you so much as bat an eye until I'm finished, I'll kill you if it's the last act I ever perform on this earth."

"Was that what you wanted?" Lorton gasped. "I thought you—"

"It seems to me that half my life I've been wanting to talk on a telephone without being gobbled up alive," January answered. "Now I've got the chance. If I were you, sweetheart—no—sit down. And stay sitting down. If anything happens to me before this call is finished, you'll find yourself with a bellyful of lead."

Lorton had half-risen from his chair. Under the pressure of the gun, he sank back again. The knowledge of power that had sat so heavily on his face was fleeing now.

"Don't move, sweetheart," January said. He dialed the number, spoke, "Direct connection to the chief of the FSB. January calling."

"Yes, sir." The phone clicked. He watched the stone on the ring that Atkinson had once owned. If a tinge of red appeared, he fully intended to empty the gun into Lorton's body. The stone remained dull and lifeless. An instant later he was pouring out into the phone everything that had happened. Or trying to. If he was too incoherent to make sense, he couldn't help it.

"Where are you, January?" the chief spoke.

"Chicago."

"Where in Chicago?"

He gave the address.

"Stay put," the chief said. "I'll have somebody there to

help you in ten minutes."

"Ten minutes?" Speed such as this was not to be expected even from the FSB. "When we learned that Atkinson was missing, we started looking for you. When your partial message came through, we started looking even harder. I've got twenty men in Chicago right now looking for you, and more on the way. I've got a mobile radio unit in operation there now. My men are carrying miniature receivers. They'll be on their way to you as soon as I put your address on the air. Hold on, January. Help is on the way."

"I'll hold on."

The first agent arrived in seven minutes. The others came later.

They came fast and left even faster. January insisted on it. "We got to get him to some place where we can talk to him in safety." He pointed to the dazed Lorton on the other side of the desk. "To do that, we got to move fast. If we don't move fast enough, the chances are we'll never move at all."

What he meant was, they had to get away before the Brain sent a *penth* to find out what was going on. They had Lorton. But they didn't have the Brain.

"We got the head of a snake," January said. "But this snake has a worse stinger in this tail than in the fangs in his mouth. Move."

They moved. When they went out they took Lorton with them.

CHAPTER EIGHT

WHEN THE New Federal Building had been constructed in Chicago in 1960 the architects had carried out one aspect of governmental building policy that had been in effect for over a decade, namely, as nearly as possible to make all government buildings atom bomb proof.

There is, of course, no such thing as a building that is proof against a direct hit by an atom bomb. At the terrific temperatures generated by the fission of plutonium, stone and metal simply volatize, but certain precautions can be taken against a near miss, of which depth and concrete in the order named are the most important.

In constructing this building, depth had been achieved simply by digging deep and the concrete had been poured from a lavish hand. The building, impregnable against ordinary attack, was the safest structure in Chicago. At the deepest level there was maintained an elaborate set of offices, a large-scale testing laboratory, and a communication network that could reach every corner of the United States. Stored water, stored food, and its own electrical generating system would allow the occupants of the sub-surface levels to exist indefinitely without contact with the outside world. Carefully disguised steel doors barred entrance to the lower levels.

In an office in the lower level of this building five men were in conference. One was Warren Carter, chief of the Federal Security Bureau. A military rocket plane had flown him in from Washington. He had brought with him an assistant. The third member of the group was Rick Blackstone, Federal Bureau of Investigation agent-in-charge of the Chicago District. He also had an assistant with him. The fifth member of the group was Joe January.

Although it made no difference here, night had long since fallen outside. January had had a shave, a bath. Food and clean clothes had made him feel so much better that he was almost willing to stay alive.

From where he sat in the office, he could look through an open door and see in a laboratory a man who was most unhappy. The man was Giles Lorton.

Lorton was getting his lumps.

For hours, agents had been questioning him. They had gotten no information beyond the bare statement of his name, age, and address. Lorton had spent his time yelling for his lawyer. His fingerprints had been taken and were now being checked in an effort to discover who he actually was.

Lorton was quite a mystery to the agents. The big question was how he had gotten control of the Brain.

There were other questions about Lorton and since he refused to answer any of them, the lab technicians were preparing to use pentathal on him. Under the influence of this "truth drug" a man coughed up his guts.

CARTER, the FSB chief, was squirming over the necessity of using this drug not only because the evidence thus gathered could not be used in court but also because Lorton's lawyers would yell to high heaven that the third degree had been used on their client, but Carter, even though he was squirming, was prepared to go ahead and order the use of the drug. He had to do it. It was vitally important for them to learn what Lorton knew and that as quickly as possible.

Without his help, they couldn't even locate the Brain.

Given time, they could locate it, but days or weeks might be required. They didn't have weeks to spend, they didn't have days, maybe they didn't even have hours.

Nancy Howe was missing. She had not reported to the police, to the FBI, or to the FSB. It was possible, of course, that she had not as yet dared to report, but it was also possible that the Brain had finally succeeded in locating her and that, under the threat of a *penth,* she was being held captive.

Every time he thought of what might have happened to her, January had to fight himself to keep from getting up and going into the lab and kicking the truth out of Lorton personally.

January could not reveal where the Brain was hidden. All he knew was that it was underground and that the miniature railway system under the Loop made contact with it but remembering how the slave engineer had used the flashlight in locating the exact spot where the door opened from the railway into the passage which led to the Brain, he knew that he would need days and maybe weeks just to find the same spot again.

He didn't want to go looking for that spot.

He didn't believe he would ever live long enough to find it.

Certain steps had been taken. A whole staff of men, working with a complete map of the underground railway system, were searching for places where the Brain might be located. Even these men were not too anxious to find the right spot.

They liked life as well as anybody else.

Other steps had also been taken. Atkinson's laboratory had been raided and every notebook, every sheet of paper, every drawing, every uncompleted piece of apparatus had been brought here. Another staff of experts was going through this material. They were also examining the little light weapon that Atkinson had tried to use on the *penth.*

January had turned the weapon over to them.

Atkinson had hoped it could be used against a *penth.*

The men in the laboratory had the same hope.

A preliminary report on the operation of the weapon had already been made to January by a sweating physicist who had been called in from the staff of a local university to investigate the light gun. "Actually, it projects a high frequency vibration field along with intense visible light. From what notes he left, Atkinson seemed to think that the tuning of the field was of the utmost importance."

The physicist was named Wishwell. He was a sweating, scared little man. Although he had repeated time and time again that he did not believe that such a thing as a *penth* existed or could exist, he was working like a fool trying to solve the secret of the light gun.

Doubt as to the existence of such things as *penths* or even the Brain itself had been expressed in other quarters. Even Carter, chief of the FSB, had been doubtful. Support of January's story had come from two different sources. The first source had been Blackstone. "I would say it's the biggest bunch of hot air I've ever seen except that we've been picking up rumors from other sources that tell the same story. In one instance we've got the report of a man who claimed he saw a black ball just as you describe these *penths* eat a living man."

AFTER BLACKSTONE had spoken, there hadn't been much more argument as to whether or not such things as *penths* could exist. A little later all argument had stopped. A report had come in from the police. "Black ball chases man down State Street. Overtaken, the man is seen to vanish. Special reserves have been called out to control the panic among the spectators."

After this report had come in, no one had really doubted January's story, not even Wishwell.

"Those damned *penths* could run everybody out of the Loop." Blackstone had muttered.

"Not as long as we've got the big shot," January answered.

He nodded toward the laboratory where Lorton was again yelling for his lawyers. "Obviously the Brain can act without his direction but it cannot take action against us as long as we have him. Lorton is the key to the whole thing. When he talks, we'll know what to do." He looked meaningfully at Carter. "Chief, the sooner you order him shot full of truth juice, the quicker we'll get to the bottom of this thing."

"Well—"

"And the better chance we'll have of staying alive. That includes you and a lot of other people, Chief." January ended.

"All right," Carter said. "But the Lord help the whole lot of us when his lawyers get us into court."

"Quit worrying. I'll give you nine to one we never see the inside of a court."

"Why not?"

"We won't live that long," January answered. "Come on. I want to watch Lorton get his hide full of truth juice. I think I'll enjoy seeing him squirm." He rose and moved into the adjoining laboratory. The whole group followed him. Lorton looked at them from apprehensive eyes.

"I demand to be allowed to talk to my attorney. I demand to know what charges are lodged against me."

"You got a lot of guts, sweetheart," January said. "Remember me? I'm the guy who saw Atkinson die. You ordered that execution, didn't you?"

Lorton goggled at him. "I—I—"

"Stick him, boys," January said to the technicians. "Dull up the needles a bit before you run them through his hide."

The technicians didn't dull the needles, but Lorton yelled as much as if they had.

The drug was slow in taking effect. Before Lorton had begun to talk, an aide from the communications department had called Carter out of the room. When the FSB chief returned, he motioned to January. "There's a man on the phone who wants to talk to you."

"To me? How the hell does he know I'm here?"

"He doesn't. The call is being relayed back from Washington. He doesn't know where you are. He says his name is Howe and that it is very important for him to talk to you."

"Howe! Holy hell!" January was already out of the room.

CLIPPED and terse, Gray Suit's voice came over the wire. "January, where are you? I've got to see you right now. Hell's broken loose for sure."

"What do you mean?"

"Something has happened to Lorton," Howe's voice came. "I don't know what happened, but something—"

"I know," January said. "We've got him."

"You've got him?"

"Tight and fast. We're starting to give him truth serum."

"The truth serum?"

"Yeah. He's mighty reluctant to talk. This dope will change his mind."

There was a moment of silence, then Howe's voice came again. "January, I've got to see you right away."

"Not so fast. I keep remembering one thing."

"What thing?"

"That you're a slave of the Brain."

A laugh sounded. "I've licked it. I've broken the chains, January. Otherwise how do you think I would be able to talk to you? January, I've got to see you right now. I know how to stop the Brain."

Desperate urgency sounded in his voice.

"How?"

"I can't tell you, over the phone. Hell's broken loose, January. The *penths* are turning this city upside down, looking for Lorton. If they don't find him, I don't know what will happen, but it may be a massacre. The Brain may herd thousands of people into some building and start killing them. It may keep right on killing them until Lorton is produced. January, I've got to see you."

"Stay right where you are and I'll have you picked up." He got the address from Howe, called the police department, had a squad car sent for the man.

Gray Suit was trembling when he was brought to the lower levels. His face was gray with globules of sweat standing out on a pasty skin. "Has Lorton talked yet?" was his first question.

"They're working on him now," January answered.

"Where—where is he?"

January nodded toward the closed door of the laboratory. A split second after he made the gesture he knew he had made a mistake, he knew that admitting this man here had been a most horrible mistake.

From the laboratory came a wild scream of a man. The door was jerked open. Five men tried to get through that door at the same instant. Through the opening thus revealed, January caught a glimpse of Lorton lying on a table.

Hissing in the air above him was a *penth*.

"You—you brought that thing here!" January gasped.

"I—I couldn't help it," Gray Suit's choked voice came. "I—I am not only a slave—forced to do as I'm told, but—but the Brain has Nancy."

"And now it has us..." January whispered. Carter, Blackstone, their aides, and the technicians from the laboratory, piled through the door. To them, the *penth* had seemed to materialize out of nowhere. When that ball of swirling blackness appeared, panic hit them.

Somewhere, in the far distance of another world, an excited man was yelling: "I've got it."

But even if he was in a panic, as he came through the door

Blackstone was pulling a gun. He had courage, did this man of the FBI. He spun around the door, faced back into the lab. The gun thundered in his hand.

The slugs probably hit the *penth*, Blackstone was too good a marksman to miss at this close range. But for all the effect they had, they might as well have missed.

The *penth* moved—toward Lorton.

JANUARY'S hair stood on end. He had expected the *penth* to move toward the fleeing men, or toward him, or in any direction except toward Lorton.

Lorton was the big shot—he was the boss. He was the ruler of the Brain.

But master or not, the *penth* was moving toward him.

Even in his drugged state, he saw the moving ball of blackness. He must have guessed its intention. Or perhaps he knew. He screamed.

The chilled mechanical voice of the brain whispered in the room.

"You fool! If you had not order-ed At-kin-son killed in the pres-ence of the FSB a-gent, this would not have happened. You made a mistake. I have no use for defective tools."

"But—wait!" Lorton screamed.

"I do not need you any longer," the mechanical voice answered. "You are a source of danger to me. You will tell everything you know. Therefore—"

The *penth* moved closer. Lorton's scream rose up, up, up, until it seemed as if his vocal chords were being ripped from his throat. Blackstone's gun thundered again. The acrid fumes of burned powder swirled through the office. The *penth* moved down, down.

It touched Lorton. Abruptly the scream went into silence. For a split second January had a glimpse of a body heaving at the straps that held it to the table, then the body was gone.

As Atkinson had gone. Gone from where it was to somewhere else. Eaten, destroyed, shoved into another space.

"Beat it!" January yelled.

It seemed to him that he became a part of a wave of men who fought their way out or the office and into the corridor outside. A *penth* had found its way into the steel and concrete underground fortress that had been designed to withstand anything except a direct hit from an atom bomb.

January had assumed that as long as they had Lorton, the Brain was licked. Not until the *penth* had materialized did he realize that Lorton, instead of being the master of the Brain, was only a tool of that monstrous structure of crystal, perhaps not quite a slave as others were—otherwise the Brain would have been able to locate him instantly—but a tool just the same.

For a time Lorton had been a useful tool. Ceasing being useful, he had been destroyed.

"We've got to get out of here!" January shouted. "We've got to get lost."

Perhaps, if they could escape, if they could find some secret hideaway, they could yet devise some method of destroying the Crystal Brain.

If they could escape.

In response to his voice, the wave of men poured down the corridor. These were tough men, hard-boiled men, tough-minded men. They would face death cheerfully, as being a part of their duty, a calculated risk they were prepared to take. But this *penth* that came out of nowhere and destroyed a man they could not face.

Not now at least. Not while panic rolled through them like a tidal wave rolling over an island. Later, when the panic had worn itself out, they would regroup and come back to face even a *penth*.

If there was a later.

A man yelled: "That damned thing is following us!"

Swirling down the corridor behind them was the *penth*.

Ahead of them a little man appeared again in the door of a lab to yell: "I've got it!" In his hand he held a little gadget.

He was Wishwell, the physicist.

He saw the tide of men pouring toward him. A look of alarm appeared on his face.

He saw the penth following them.

He had denied, indignantly, that such a thing as a *penth* could exist.

Now, for the first time, he saw one. The alarm on his face crystallized into an expression of acute panic.

"Wh—wh—what is that thing?"

"A *penth!*" someone shouted.

Wishwell lifted the little weapon that he held in his hand. The beam of light that flared from it was an intense violet in color.

CHAPTER NINE

THE GIRL heard the shots as they sounded through the loudspeaker in the room of the Brain. The sounds were coming from elsewhere, she knew, and were being transmitted back to the Brain by the unique radio system of the *penths*. She also heard the screams and the voice speaking from the Brain.

Then came the sound of running footsteps. Voices shouted. She could not make out what was being said.

What happened after that she did not know. Suddenly every clicking relay in the banked panels around the Brain went dead. A cry like nothing she had ever heard before boomed through the room.

She was busy working replacing a burned-out relay in one of the panels. After being brought here, she had been "treated" again. The treatment had not taken effect but this fact she hid on pain of sudden death. She obeyed every order she received, promptly and willingly, knowing that the first sign of disobedience would be the end of her.

At the sound of the cry, she turned her head to look at the Brain. The blackness that hung above the massed crystals was writhing. A constant stream of *penths* were materializing in the room and were flowing into it, merging themselves with it.

The blackness twisted like it was alive. The cry sounded again. It was a cry of pain, of agony, of deep hurt.

Somewhere, somehow, something had been hurt. And hurt badly. It was crying out in pain. Mixed with the wail of pain was burning anger, furious hate. The cry said that the something that had been hurt would get revenge for the pain it was suffering.

She saw the something get its revenge.

The door opened. A slave stood there. The whole ball of blackness detached itself from the top of the Brain and rolled toward the slave. He screamed and tried to draw away. The ball of blackness rolled over him, engulfed him, swallowed him up.

Something had been hurt, now it had hurt this slave, as revenge.

As though relishing the feel of the pain he had suffered, the ball of blackness hung over the spot where the slave had stood. Then it lifted and settled itself again on top of the Crystal Brain.

In that moment Nancy Howe grasped the horrible truth about the Brain. It shocked her to the bottom of her soul. It hit her as the charge of electric current hits a man strapped in the death chair, as a bolt of lightning hits a victim who has taken refuge under a tree during a thunderstorm, shocking to the point of death itself, but not killing. In this cold room she felt the bite of a deeper cold, a numbing, destroying feeling.

She knew the secret truth about the Brain.

The truth was so hideous that, as lightning striking a power line knocks out the electric lights, her mind was knocked out. She slid to the floor.

She did not know how long she was unconscious. She recovered, vaguely, at the feel of strong hands moving under her arms and lifting her. She cried out, once.

Mike's voice came, soothingly. "It's all right, sis. You just chucked a faint because of the cold in here. Just take it easy and you'll be all right."

"Oh, Mike." To her eyes the chimpanzee face looked like the features of Sir Galahad.

MIKE LIFTED her in strong arms, carried her from the

room. Another slave had already taken over her unfinished task. All around the room, the relays were chattering again. The Brain was functioning. But the relays seemed to be clicking faster now, as though driven by a rising emergency.

Whatever that emergency, the Brain seemed to be adequate to meet it.

Within the hour she saw the first steps taken to cope with that emergency. Slaves who had been hastily dispatched on some errand returned with machine guns, which they set up to cover the underground passages.

"They raided an armory," Mike managed to whisper to her. "*Penths* went in and knocked out the guards. The boys went in and helped themselves to all the guns and ammo they wanted. Nothing to it." He shrugged. "They could take the mint the same way if the Brain wanted 'em to."

"Machine guns!" She worried with the idea. "That must mean the Brain thinks we are going to be attacked. Otherwise it would not have gotten the guns."

"What else could it mean?"

"But—are we going to use those guns against our friends? I mean, if the place is attacked."

The chimpanzee face was a mass of wrinkles. "You name anything else we can do and we'll do it. We're slaves, sis. We do as we are told. Or else."

She knew what the "or else" meant. But she saw another demonstration of it. One of the men working at the big benches in the main room dropped a tool. The hissing sound came instantly. He had time to scream once. But not twice before the *penth* had him.

In the silence that followed, Mike managed to whisper. "The slightest slip from now on—and bingo!"

The irritated and apparently frightened Brain, working under pressure, had no sympathy for its human tools. Nor was it taking any chances that they would betray it.

She looked always for her brother, but did not find him. She did not dare ask questions, except to Mike, and from him all she got was a shrug and the whispered statement that her brother had been sent somewhere.

As soon as the machine guns were set up, the slaves were assembled in the main chamber and set to work building something, what they did not know. The parts that went into it were improvised from the equipment on hand. Radio transmitting tubes were brought up from the storerooms, other equipment assembled.

"It's a weapon of some kind," Mike whispered.

"But what about the machine guns? I should think they would be enough, the guns and the *penths*. What else could be needed?"

"I don't know," Mike answered. "The Brain seems to think something else is needed or it wouldn't have us building this."

"What kind of a weapon is it?"

"I'm scared to think," the little man answered.

THEY SOON learned what the weapon did. A cone of wires was set up on top of the construction. Like a radar antenna, it could be swung to point in any direction. When the weapon was finished, a slave was ordered to stand to one side.

The radar cone, under the direct operation of the Brain, swung around to point at the man. Out from it lashed—nothing. Or nothing that could be seen. But the slave exploded. Bits of battered flesh, blood, fragments of bone, spattered the walls. Steam puffed violently outward. The stench was sickening.

"It's a ray of some kind," Mike muttered. "Turns the body fluids into super-heated steam." He mused darkly. "God, I'd hate to be one of the boys who come in here to try to take the Brain. If the *penths* or the machine guns don't get 'em, this damned thing will."

Nancy Howe was violently sick. A heavy wrench caught her eye. She picked it up. Mike, sensing her attention, grabbed her arm, held it.

"Don't be stupid, sis. If you throw that wrench, sure, you'll bust the tubes in that damned weapon, but after a *penth* has taken care of you, me and some of the boys will put in new tubes. You won't gain anything."

He broke off. Somewhere in the near vicinity a muffled blast had sounded. Under their feet the concrete floor trembled.

Far-off, a voice yelled. "Okay, boys, the door's down. Come on. We're going in."

"They've blasted the door that leads to the underground railway," Mike whispered. "The police, or somebody, is coming." Exultation sounded in his voice. He had lived for this day, for this hour, when he would be a slave no longer.

So had all the others. Hope, like a living flame, ran through the room.

Mike's exultation was short-lived. "To the machine guns!" the orders of the Brain pounded through the room. Mike, and the others moved to obey.

The cone on top of the ray projector swung around to face the passage from which the attack must come.

Nancy Howe threw the wrench.

It struck in the middle of the bank of tubes that energized the weapon. Broken glass splashed outward. Filaments, suddenly oxidizing in air, flared red, then burned white, then went out in little puffs of smoke.

With the filaments burned out, the ray projector would not function.

Nancy Howe threw herself backward into the nearest room, quickly but silently closed the door. She lay flat on the floor, shivering. There was just a chance that the attention of the Brain was so completely concentrated on the emergency of the explosion that it had not seen who threw the tool that wrecked the ray projector.

The Brain might not have the opportunity to hunt for the guilty person.

In that case, she had a chance to stay alive.

Otherwise, at any moment, a *penth* would materialize above her head and that would be the end of her, the end of Nancy Howe, who as Nancy Howard, had tried to solve the mystery of Giles Lorton and the Crystal Brain.

She closed her eyes and tried to pray.

Outside, she heard the chatter of the machine guns begin.

CHAPTER TEN

WHEN THE first machine gun slug went past his head, Joe January ducked back out of the passage that led to the underground quarters of the Brain.

"Everybody back," he yelled.

He had not expected to find machine guns here. When he had been here before, there had been no guns in sight. *Penths*, yes. *Penths* by the dozens, *penths* by the hundreds. But no machine-guns. He had expected slaves, such as William Henry Howe, now confined in a straitjacket and under complete sedation in a hospital, to try to fight the attackers. The Brain had tried to call Howe back to it, after Lorton was killed. He had put up a stiff fight before he was overcome. January expected the slaves here to put up an equally stiff fight.

Machine gun slugs howled past them, smashing into the concrete wall on the other side of the railroad.

"For crying out loud…what are those things?" a fretful little man quavered. It was Wishwell, the physicist, who asked the question. Wishwell had never heard a machine gun in operation and did not know how one sounded.

Blackstone explained to him.

"Gas masks!" January shouted. Even though he had not expected to find machine guns here, he had a way to deal with them. At his order, dozens of men spread along the track of the railroad began to don masks.

"Okay, roll her up," The FSB agent ordered. In response to the command, a car of the miniature railway began to edge closer to the opening the explosion had made. Powerful lights were mounted on the car. The engineer of the locomotive was not one of the regular employees of the railroad. No regular employee was at work today. The operating group had been replaced, suddenly, with absolutely no explanation given, as soon as they reported for their work duties. January was taking no chances on having a railroad worker who was also a slave of the Brain report what was in progress. He remembered too well the Irish engineer who had taken them out of the place when they were fleeing from the Brain.

He was taking no chances at all, if he could help it. Every contingency that could be anticipated had been anticipated, he hoped.

The car stopped. It did not quite reach the opening that had been blown in the wall. In the back of it a man stood up. With a short-barreled gun, he began firing into the tunnel. The gun he was using did not explode; it went off with a heavy *phut!* He fired at an angle into the opening, firing contact shells that exploded on impact and released a flood of invisible odorless gas.

When he started firing, machine gun slugs still howled from the opening. At the second shot, a yell sounded inside. It was a choked yell. At the third shot, the machine gun stopped, abruptly, then started again.

January, crouching against the wall and fitting the mask over his face, could almost see what had happened inside. The gunner had got himself a snoot-full of gas and had gone down. A second man had pulled him away from the gun and had taken his place.

The gun stopped again.

"Second gunner gone," January said. He started up, then pulled back down as another machine gun began firing.

THE GAS gunner in the railroad car was methodically reloading the short, big-barreled gas weapon. He began to fire again, pouring a flood of the heavy bursting shells into the tunnel. The second machine gun went into silence.

Leaning over the car, the gunner called down. "Give that gas five minutes to take effect."

January nodded, looked at his watch. Blackstone, Wishwell, and Carter moved up close to him. "You're running this show, Joe," Carter said. "You say when we go."

"We'll go now," January said, checking his watch. "The mop-up squads will follow right behind us." In both directions, the railroad tunnel seemed full of men. Overhead, on the surface, January knew other men were taking up their places. A complete cordon was being thrown around this spot. Squad cars and ambulances were ready, copters were hovering overhead.

Once they had located the hiding place of the Brain, it had been possible to plan decisive action.

No human being could escape from this spot. Those who tried would be held for rigorous examination, and if they were slaves of the Brain, they would be hospitalized.

January picked up his hat, which he had removed while donning the gas mask, tossed it into the opening. No shot came. He climbed up.

Ahead, at the intersection of the passages, he saw two machine guns; the gunner slumped down over the weapons.

"Come on," he called to the men behind him.

They came. Something else came too. A *penth*!

At the sight of the ball of blackness, his flesh crawled. This, he knew, was it. He lifted the little weapon he held.

Atkinson's weapon. This was the only name they had for it. The weapon that Atkinson had invented and that Wishwell had perfected in the nick of time. The weapon that had stopped the *penth* that Howe had brought into the sub basement of the Federal Building. Would it stop this *penth* as it had stopped the other one?

The *penth* moved toward him.

Atkinson's weapon flared with its beam of intolerable brilliance. Violet light shot outward.

The *penth* tried to dodge, tried to come on, tried to lift above the beam, tried to duck below it. For an instant, the light weapon and the blob of darkness fenced like two swordsmen in some incredible duel from some fantastic nightmare. Facing the beam of violet light, the penth began to moan. It was in pain and the pain was voiced as a shrill whine that protested against this intolerable beam of light, wailing that the light hurt it.

January enjoyed that whine of pain. He remembered how Atkinson had screamed, how Lorton had begged for mercy. Lorton had got what was coming to him but Atkinson had been a gentle, kindly old man, whose one thought had been research with the ultimate goal of improving the lot of the human race. Atkinson had gotten no mercy. So far as January was concerned, no *penth* from the Crystal Brain was going to get any mercy from him.

Abruptly the whine died. The *penth* vanished. Whether it had been destroyed or whether it had returned to the Brain in the sub-dimensional transit that was the normal mode of travel of these creatures, January could not tell. All he knew was that it was gone.

At the moment, nothing else mattered. Atkinson's weapon had held up, had won a victory. January and every other man here had bet their lives on that weapon.

BEHIND him, Blackstone, Wishwell, and Carter were scrambling up into the passage. Behind them were the mop-up squads, organized like an army, with everything from fighters to stretcher-bearers to take care of any casualties, also to begin the task of hurrying the slaves out of this place of horror to hospitals where they could secure treatment to release them from their bondage.

"Let's go," January said.

They moved forward.

Where the connecting passages met, machine gun slugs filled the air again. They waited while the gas gun was brought up. When the guns were silent, they went forward again.

"There's a girl here," January spoke to the leader of the first mop-up squad. "Before you bother with anybody else, try to find her."

"I'll do my best."

Although January didn't know it then, the girl who was here had saved his life the instant he passed the corner. It was on this spot that the ray weapon had been focused.

They reached the big chamber in front of the room that housed the Brain. Here—among the slaves—Mike slept quietly over his machine gun. The wrinkled face of the little chimpanzee man indicated he was enjoying this sleep, perhaps for the first time in years. Here, also, they saw the ray weapon that had been improvised.

They hadn't seen another *penth*.

"I don't like it," Carter muttered. "I don't like it a little."

Neither did January. But he didn't say anything.

Ahead was the heavy steel door blocking the way to the room of the Crystal Brain. Behind steel and concrete, the Brain seemed secure.

"Bring up the cutting torches," January ordered.

On the run, a squad of men moved forward. They brought with them the most advanced cutting equipment, torches that would cut through tungsten steel as if it was butter.

The steel door was attacked.

"Indians!" Blackstone yelled. "Look out!"

As the cutting torches began to eat into the door, the air suddenly boiled with *penths*. They came from nowhere, blurring as they sprang into existence, black balls of nothingness, hissing their anger and their defiance. No human being had ever defied them before. Some of the men facing them now had run from them once.

But ran no longer! They would run once, but they came of a fighting breed, and they would not run twice.

The Brain hurled forth its entire force of demons.

Beams of violet light flashed up to meet them. *Penths* twisted, evaded, squirmed, wailed that death was a horrible thing, slid into nothingness to dodge the torturing light, emerged again from nothingness and kept coming.

Members of the mop-up squads, armed with Atkinson's light weapon, moved up quickly to join the fight around the steel door.

The first *penth* victory was scored against a mop-up squad man. His light weapon failed.

He screamed. A split second later, he had ceased to exist.

The second man screamed. A *penth* had gotten in under his guard and had wiped him out of existence.

The third man did not scream. Simply ceasing to exist, he did not have time to energize his vocal chords.

Out of the corner of his eyes, January caught a glimpse of the third man vanishing. Not for the first time, but perhaps for the hundredth time, it occurred to him that they were not going to win this fight.

"Hurry up with that door!" he shouted.

"We're going as fast as we can," a torch man answered.

THE TOUGH steel did not run like butter. As the minutes passed and the *penths* hissed in undiminished numbers, coming out of nothingness and dodging back into it almost too fast for the eye to follow, more and more Joe January began to realize that the winning of this fight depended on their getting through that steel door.

Once through the door, he had something in his pocket that would smash the Crystal Brain. With the Brain gone, the *penths* either would not exist or would be without control.

Wishwell, Carter, Blackstone, and January stood back to back, protecting themselves and the men with the cutting torches.

"We can't take much more of this," Carter gasped.

He spoke truer than he knew. A *penth,* materializing at floor level, struck upward before the FSB chief could lower the light weapon. Striking upward, the *penth* wiped Carter out of existence as one wipes a mark from a slate with a wet sponge.

With a crash, the steel door went down.

Cold air puffed out. Inside, January caught a glimpse of the Crystal Brain squatting under its cloud of blackness, heard a continuous clicking of relays so loud it was almost a roar.

From his coat pocket, January lifted the hand grenade he had brought along for this moment, if the moment ever arrived. It had arrived. He pulled the firing pin with his teeth, tossed the grenade into the room of the Brain, shouted two words.

"One side!"

The torchmen were already moving back and away. Blackstone, January, and Wishwell moved with them, protecting them from the darting *penths* that came and went like balls of black lightning.

The grenade exploded in a flash of flame and a thundering burst of sound. Beneath their feet, the concrete floor jumped. Came the tinkle of breaking plastic, like the crash of windowpanes breaking and the glass breaking as it fell to the sidewalk. January found himself holding his breath waiting not for a new sound but for the absence of an old one.

There was a split second of silence. Men and *penths* alike seemed to be holding their breath, waiting.

The absence of sound came. January sighed. The relays were silent. This was the silence he had been waiting to hear, the silence that told him the Brain had been smashed.

"It's gone, it's done," he heard his own voice say. Inside he was aware of a tremendous surge of psychic relief. The abominable Brain was smashed, finished, done. In this one instance, at least, something that all scientists seemed to fear had ceased to exist.

At the same moment when he realized the relays were silent and the Brain smashed, he also realized that something else was wrong. He needed a second to grasp where the wrongness lay. Then he got it. The *penths* ought to have disappeared. When the Brain ceased to function they should either have gone out of existence or they should have begun to drift aimlessly. Now that the Brain was gone, nothing was directing, was it?

But they hadn't disappeared.

They weren't drifting out of control.

Very subtly their movements had changed when the Brain was smashed. They were no longer appearing and disappearing. They seemed to remain continuously in existence. Their speed was perhaps a little slower but they were still very much present.

Present enough to strike down and destroy a mop-up man who had momentarily relaxed his guard.

And—at the sight, January's heart climbed up in his throat and threatened to choke him—out of the room of the shattered Crystal Brain was coming—the great grand-daddy of all the *penths* that had ever existed.

BESIDE HIM he heard Blackstone choke and gulp. "Hell's out for noon sure. Here comes the devil himself to see what we've been doing to his little demons."

The ball that came out of the room of the Brain was at

least three feet in diameter. It swirled, sluggishly, with an ugly blackness. It was the same darkness that had squatted over the top of the Crystal Brain.

In this moment Joe January realized what Nancy Howe had said earlier, that it was not the Brain itself that was their enemy, it was this creature of darkness, this thing, this alien, this whatever it was.

A man named Michaelson had invented the Crystal Brain. January had finally learned about Michaelson, that eccentric genius who was perhaps the world's foremost authority on digital calculators, on mechanical brains. Men had been forced to invent brains to aid in solving the mathematical problems that a mechanical brain could solve in a few hours but which would take a man years to solve.

Michaelson had gone farther, by far, than anyone else in this field of research. He had created the Crystal Brain. The network of relays behind the panels were the controls, the memory, the storage tanks for the information that was housed and integrated in the Brain itself. The Brain had been the core of his life's work. This had been his secret laboratory where he had worked for years. Here he had created the Brain.

And something else had taken over the operation of his invention. Squatting on top of the Brain, this something else controlled it, worked through it.

In this frozen moment Joe January tried to think what this something else might possibly be. He knew it was life, some form of life hitherto unknown on earth, unless, perhaps, it was the life-form that the Druid priests had worshipped and tried to evoke in the circle of gigantic stones at Stonehenge, that the priests of the upper Nile had sensed existed, and had named the Lord of the Underworld. Perhaps neither of these ideas were altogether correct. Joe January didn't really think they were. He thought this thing, this alien, was actually a creature of far-distant interstellar space that had wandered earthward and had discovered in Michaelson's Crystal Brain the tool it needed to contact, and—*control*, the inhabitants of this planet.

All scientists had seemed to sense this thing, or something like it, might exist, and that their probing telescopes would someday discover it. They had been afraid they might find this thing.

Whatever it was—*it was!*

It came floating out of the room of the Brain as high as a man's head. Wordless signals seemed to flash from It, signals that the *penths* understood and obeyed. Instantly every *penth* in the room flashed toward the ball, disappeared into it, blending their substance with it.

As the *penths* disappeared into it, it grew larger.

As he saw the *penths* vanish and the ball of blackness enlarge, January realized at last that the *penths* were not products of the Brain, they were products or this alien, they were part of it, sum and substance identical with it, parts of its body that it detached and sent to do its bidding. Perhaps the control of the distant *penths* was made more effective through the radio signals that flowed out from the Brain and out from the big transmitter in this room, but the *penths* were never creatures of the Brain.

They were bits of this body of this alien creature.

It hung in the air before them, blacker than midnight, hissing with the threat of a thousand cobras.

It moved toward them.

PANIC HIT the men in the room. Here was something they had never seen before and had never imagined. Here was the devil himself come up out of darkest hell to devour them. Somewhere a man yelled, a sound ripped from a throat in the depths of mortal terror. "Knock that fool down," January said.

It was Blackstone who leaped and struck the panic-stricken man as he started to run. If one had run, others would have run too. If you stop the first one, you may stop all of them.

January stood his ground. He could feel sweat pouring out of him in leprous patches. Cold from the ball of blackness washed over him. He knew only one thing—he wasn't going to run.

He lifted the light weapon.

"This one is for you, Atkinson," he whispered, and pressed the trigger.

Out shot the flare of violet light.

The ball of darkness flinched. Whatever it was, the violet light hurt it.

The room seemed to blaze with blinding brilliance as men leaped to stand beside January, to join him in pouring the hated violet radiation into the grand-daddy of all *penths*.

For a second, it kept coming. Then it flinched and tried to draw away. Given an instant, perhaps it would have succeeded in dematerializing itself as did the *penths*. But it didn't have that instant. It didn't have any time whatsoever.

Suddenly, while the lights poured into it, it began to fall apart.

The room moaned with sound. Something that had come from interstellar space was wailing that now it would never again reach its far-off home, that in its wanderings it had run across a race that had seemed to be pygmies, little creatures of no importance.

Only they weren't pygmies. They were giants. They were prepared to hold their world against all *penths*. They were destroying this one.

The darkness broke apart, seemed to run like oil, flowed, felt for the first time the grip of gravity, and began to flow downward like a wet spray of falling oil.

It lost all coherence, all resemblance to a ball. With the loss of form, the moan went into silence.

Still the lights beat into it.

Like tiny bits of carbon black, it fell to the floor. It left there only an oily smudge of nothingness.

It was gone.

In the room there was not a single sound. No man breathed, no man moved, no man whispered. Each of them knew in his secret heart that here the human race had come up against one of the horrors of hell's far distant spaces, and had emerged triumphant.

Joe January sat down on the floor. It seemed to him he no longer had the strength to stand. Around him men were beginning to move and to talk, blabbering questions, wanting to know what that thing had been, where it had come from, how it had worked. Let 'em blabber, he thought. They'll work it out to their own satisfaction, they'll think of something. He hardly heard them.

Running footsteps sounded. He looked up. A girl stood there. Her lips moved. "Joe. Joe January." He hardly heard her, hardly remembered that she existed. Who was she?

Then, as he remembered where and under what circumstances he had first met and talked to her—presuming that a whispered conversation in the dark counted as talk—he remembered who she was. His fingers went into tile pocket of his coat seeking a cigarette. And little by little, a grin began to form on his face.

THE END

If you've enjoyed this book, you will not want to miss these terrific titles...

ARMCHAIR SCI-FI & HORROR DOUBLE NOVELS, $12.95 each

D-71   **THE DEEP END** by Gregory Luce
        TO WATCH BY NIGHT by Robert Moore Williams

D-72   **SWORDSMAN OF LOST TERRA** by Poul Anderson
        PLANET OF GHOSTS by David V. Reed

D-73   **MOON OF BATTLE** by J. J. Allerton
        THE MUTANT WEAPON by Murray Leinster

D-74   **OLD SPACEMEN NEVER DIE!** John Jakes
        RETURN TO EARTH by Bryan Berry

D-75   **THE THING FROM UNDERNEATH** by Milton Lesser
        OPERATION INTERSTELLAR by George O. Smith

D-76   **THE BURNING WORLD** by Algis Budrys
        FOREVER IS TOO LONG by Chester S. Geier

D-77   **THE COSMIC JUNKMAN** by Rog Phillips
        THE ULTIMATE WEAPON by John W. Campbell

D-78   **THE TIES OF EARTH** by James H. Schmitz
        CUE FOR QUIET by Thomas L. Sherred

D-79   **SECRET OF THE MARTIANS** by Paul W. Fairman
        THE VARIABLE MAN by Philip K. Dick

D-80   **THE GREEN GIRL** by Jack Williamson
        THE ROBOT PERIL by Don Wilcox

ARMCHAIR SCIENCE FICTION CLASSICS, $12.95 each

C-25   **THE STAR KINGS**
        by Edmond Hamilton

C-26   **NOT IN SOLITUDE**
        by Kenneth Gantz

C-32   **PROMETHEUS II**
        by S. J. Byrne

ARMCHAIR SCI-FI & HORROR GEMS SERIES, $12.95 each

G-7   **SCIENCE FICTION GEMS, Vol. Four**
       Jack Sharkey and others

G-8   **HORROR GEMS, Vol. Four**
       Seabury Quinn and others